The Old Man and the Marathon

A novel by

Joe C. Ellis

Upper Ohio Valley Books

Upper Ohio Valley Books
Joe C. Ellis
71299 Skyview Drive
Martins Ferry, OH 43935
Phone: 1-740-633-0423
Email: joecellis@comcast.net
www.joecellis.com

ISBN : 978-0-9796655-6-1
Printed in the U.S.A.
First printing, September 2013

PUBLISHER'S NOTE

CATALOGING INFORMATION
Ellis, Joe C., 1956-
The Old Man and the Marathon by Joe C. Ellis
ISBN 978-0-9796655-6-1
1.Pittsburgh—Fiction. 2. Wheeling, WV—Fiction
3. Martins Ferry, Ohio—Fiction 4. Sports—Fiction 5. Inspirational—Fiction.
6.Running--Fiction

Attention Filmmakers, Editors, and Publishers: If you are interested in Film/Television Rights, Foreign Rights, or American Publishing Rights to *The Old Man and the Marathon*, please contact:

Joe C. Ellis
71299 Skyview Drive
Martins Ferry, Ohio 43935

Acknowledgments

The author would like to thank the following people for their help:

Gretchen Snodgrass has done an excellent job carefully editing this novel. This is the sixth book she has edited for me, and I am always amazed at her ability to catch errors, both in grammar and plausibility. Also chipping in with editing contributions were my daughters, Rebekah Ellis Shirley and Dr. Sarah Ellis Taylor. Two good friends and running buddies also helped with corrections and insights: Kelly Kish Owens and Chrissy Martin Lewis. God bless all of you.

This book is modeled after Ernest Hemingway's *The Old Man and the Sea*. Hemingway is one of my favorite classic writers. His story of an old man taking on the challenge of trying to land a huge marlin in a small fishing boat and then facing the test of endurance as he tries to bring the fish home was the perfect framework on which to build this novel. I tried to "listen" to Hemingway's prose and dialogue as I wrote the book, hoping to reflect a small flavor of his writing style.

A Note to Readers

All my novels are now available in ebook form from Amazon.com (Kindle) and Barnesandnoble.com (Nook). If you enjoyed *The Old Man and the Marathon*, please email your friends and tell them about it. Also, I would like to hear from you. Email me with any comments or questions at joecellis@comcast.net and visit my website at www.joecellis.com.

Thanks for checking out my other novels,

Joe C. Ellis

The Healing Place by Joe C. Ellis

The rural community of Scotch Ridge on the outskirts of Martins Ferry, Ohio is a safe haven from the dangers and corruption of the world until the day Nathan Kyler arrives. He has envisioned a diabolic plan—an obsession to sacrifice another human being. His target is Christine Butler, the preacher's daughter. Soon after Christine disappears, the community rallies to find her. A mile from the Scotch Ridge Church deep in the Appalachian woods is a spot known as the Healing Place. Here something incredible happens. Available in hardcopy and ebook for Kindle and Nook.

Murder at Whalehead by Joe C. Ellis

On the northern Outer Banks looms an old hunting lodge known as the Whalehead Club. During the roaring twenties Edward and Marie Knight entertained prominent guests at this isolated Mansion by the Sea. Now it has become one of North Carolina's leading tourist attractions. Less than a quarter mile away deep in the marsh along the Currituck Sound lies the body of a young woman. Someone has killed and craves to kill again. The Butler family never expected to cross paths with a homicidal maniac while vacationing at the beach.

Available in hardcopy and ebook for Kindle and Nook

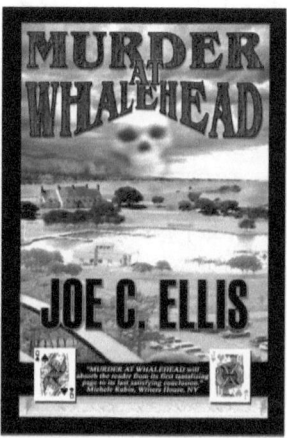

The First Shall Be Last by Joe C. Ellis

Two young lovers separated by war cling to hope and sanity by exchanging passionate letters. As Howard heads for his first battle on the Pacific island of Peleliu, Helen fulfills her call of duty by working at a local factory. They discover they have more to worry about than the Japanese forces deeply entrenched on the island. A platoon member, Judd Stone, seeks revenge against a black Marine named Josiah Jackson. Howard fears Stone may go to any length to get what he wants, even murder. Available in hardcopy and ebook for Kindle and Nook

Murder on the Outer Banks by Joe C. Ellis

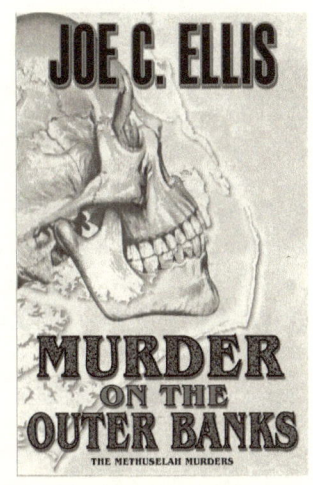

Newly hired deputy, Marla Easton, and Sheriff Dugan Walton are amazed at the performance of Dr. Sylvester Hopkins in a local 5K footrace. At sixty-five years old, Hopkins posts a world class time of 17:35, two minutes faster than he has run in the past few years. Walton suspects Hopkins has concocted some new performance enhancing drug. A trail of bodies from Frisco to Nags Head lead Deputy Easton and Sheriff Walton to the discovery of the Methuselah serum—a new drug designed by Hopkins that reverses aging in human cells. A nefarious triumvirate of pharmaceutical CEOs known as the Medical Mafia wants the formulae at any price. So does the FBI and the President of the United States. But Sheriff Walton believes that he and Deputy Easton have been divinely chosen to guard the formula and serum. Like the angels posted in Eden to guard the Tree of Life, they take their mission seriously. That mission turns perilous when Marla's seven-year-old son, Gabe, is kidnapped. Available in hardcopy, ebook for Kindle and Nook, and audiobook at Amazon.com and Audible.com.

Murder at Hatteras by Joe C. Ellis

Gabe and Marla Easton move to Hatteras Island on North Carolina's Outer Banks to escape from a stress-filled world in hopes of conceiving their first child. Shortly after their arrival, a brutal rape and murder occurs on the island. As the investigation proceeds, the Eastons are drawn into the search for the killer. Soon, everybody seems to exhibit suspicious behavior. They have no idea of the terror that awaits as they move closer to identifying the killer. Available in hardcopy and ebook for Kindle and Nook

One Season of Our lives by Joe C. Ellis
Publishing date: October 2013
Members of an Ohio high school cross country team come of age as they take on the challenge of winning the state championship. Girls, drug dealers, and death threaten to unravel this golden season. Through trial and tragedy they struggle to keep the team united and on track to achieve their goal. Along the way, team captains, Byron Butler and Will Wright, discover how one season can have a profound impact on the rest of their lives. Available in hardcopy and ebook for Kindle and Nook—

Coming in May of 2014: Murder at Ocracoke

He was an old man who lived along the banks of the Ohio River, and he had gone eighty-four days now without missing a run. In the first forty days a boy had run with him. But when high school cross country season neared, the boy's parents told him the old man held him back, and the boy had gone at their orders to the summer conditioning club with the older boys who ran faster miles. It made the boy sad to see the old man running alone each day in the heat of the summer, and he always went down to greet him with a cup of water to pour over his head. The old man's t-shirt would be soaked with sweat, the lettering and logo from a long-ago local 5K faded, and the material threadbare, with small holes in places.

The old man was thin but muscular with deep wrinkles scoring his forehead and cheeks. Brown age spots dotted and splotched his face, the consequence of many hours of training in direct sunlight. The spots also patterned his forearms and legs. Covered with sweat, his skin resembled the surface of weathered sandstone after a summer shower. To the boy he seemed ancient like the bronze statue of the World War I soldier in the city park.

Everything about him was old except for his eyes which were bright and blue, the same color as the July sky, hopeful and victorious.

"Angelo," the boy said to him as they climbed the steep steps to the old man's front porch. "I can run with you tomorrow. Our conditioning club doesn't meet on Sundays."

The old man had run with the boy since he was a child and the boy loved him.

"No," the old man said. "You're running with young lions now. Train with them."

"But remember years ago when you trained me for my first race? I won my age group and beat many of the older boys."

"I remember," the old man said. "I trained you well, but now you have a new coach."

"My father insists I follow Coach Silvers' program and run the high school workouts."

"I know," the old man said. "It makes sense."

"My father doesn't understand how much running knowledge you have. He thinks Coach Silvers is so great because he ran the Boston Marathon."

"Maybe he is."

"You don't have to run the marathon to have great knowledge, do you?"

"No," the old man said. "Training knowledge comes with experience, many miles and many races. I have plenty of that, don't I?"

"Yes," the boy said. "More than anyone I know. Can I get you a beer from your refrigerator? You can drink it on the porch and tell me about your next race."

"Why not," the old man said. "And get yourself a soda."

🏃🏃🏃🏃🏃

They sat on the front porch and many steelworkers passed by in their cars, waved, and shouted. Some hollered, "Hey, you old sonovabitch!" But the old man didn't get angry. Most of them were his friends, men he had worked with for years before he retired. He knew they envied him because he no longer had to toil before a hot blast furnace. He had worked in that hell for thirty-five years, turning iron ore into pig iron and then into steel. He had spent his days trudging through expansive buildings clad in heavy work clothes, boots, gloves, hardhat, and goggles. To Angelo, it seemed he had daily entered Dante's inferno, dark caverns lit by molten metal pouring from giant buckets hoisted high above him. The air, hot and thick with steam and fumes, had choked him, and the grease and dirt had covered any exposed skin. He did not miss the mill.

When the wind blew from the north, the smell of sulfur and the gray cast of smoke drifted through his neighborhood, but today only a slight hint could be detected in the air because the breeze came mainly from the west. The sunshine and cloudless sky made sitting on the porch and drinking a beer pleasant.

"Angelo?" the boy said.

"Yes," said the old man, holding his bottle of beer and thinking about the days when he could run ten miles under sixty minutes.

"Can I time you on tomorrow's intervals?"

"No. Go to church and spend time with your family. I have my watch."

"But I want to go. If I can't run with you, at least I could time you."

"You bring me water when I finish a run and you get me beer from my refrigerator. You've helped me for many years."

"How old was I when you first took me on a run?"

"Five, and you were nearly killed when we crossed the street, and a man driving a pickup truck didn't see us. Do you remember?"

"I can remember the tires screeching and you pulling me out of the way. I stumbled and fell back to the curb. Then I heard the sound of you pounding on the hood and yelling at the man. I thought you were going to punch him in the face."

"Do you really remember or are you recalling the story from one of the many times I've told it?"

"I remember every detail. I'll never forget."

The old man gazed at him with his cheerful blue eyes. "If you were my son, we'd go on long runs together and I'd make sure you did the proper speed and hill training. But you belong to your father and mother, and I have no right to impose."

"Please let me time you tomorrow. Where are you going to do your intervals?"

"At the high school track. Half-mile repeats. Eight of them."

"Why so much speed?"

"You must work on your weaknesses. The older I get, the slower I get."

"And you don't race farther than a 5K."

"That's true," the old man said. He did not mind difficult speed work, the burn of oxygen debt deep in the muscles and heaviness of lactic acid build up. Most grandmaster runners avoided shorter intervals out of fear of quad strains and hamstring pulls. He dove right in like an obsessed tri-athlete greeting the bone-numbing chill of the river in May.

"Will you ever race farther?"

"Maybe. But you know my problem."

"Sciatica," the boy said.

"That's right."

"When you run too far it makes your leg hurt and go numb. Is that why you can't run a marathon?"

"I'll never say never. But it would be risky."

"What could happen?"

"I could become paralyzed."

"You shouldn't do it then."

"I haven't given up the idea, but I am an old man."

"But you're strong," the boy said. "You can still run a 5K under twenty minutes."

The old man nodded and smiled, proud of his racing times, but never running a marathon always cast a shadow of inferiority on his accomplishments. "There are other training methods that could make the marathon possible for me."

4

"Really? What kind of methods?"

"Follow me," the old man said, placing his beer bottle on the banister.

They walked around the side of the house to the unattached garage. The old man opened the wooden door, entered, and flipped on the light. The walls were exposed two by fours covered on the outside with pine planks, and many cobwebs hung from the ceiling rafters. An old Dodge Duster sat in the middle with rusted fenders. A bench press, the bench cushion repaired in several places with duct tape, occupied a dark corner with the barbell resting on the two racks.

"Weight lifting?" the boy asked.

"No. Weight lifting helps, but it could never substitute for running." The old man pointed at the opposite wall. Mounted on two hooks, a racing bike hung there so covered with dust it blended into the brown background.

"Is that a Trek?"

The old man nodded. "Bought it twenty years ago."

"I didn't know you rode a bike."

"After my serious sciatica problem I had to find another method of training. Rode it for eight years until I could run long distance again."

"Eight years, that's a long time. How did you get sciatica?"

The old man smiled, the deep wrinkles scoring his cheeks. "Training for my first marathon. On a twenty mile run I lost all feeling in my right leg and crotch. I couldn't walk. The emergency squad took me to the hospital."

The boy's eyes filled with sympathy. "I see. Now you know better to try that kind of training again."

"Yes, but I'm wondering."

"Wondering what?"

"I've gone eighty-four days without any sciatica pain whatsoever. I'm wondering if I'm finally healed."

"Can sciatica be healed?"

"Over many years the nerves re-grow, find new paths."

5

The boy rubbed his smooth chin. "Healed enough to train for the marathon again?"

"We'll see." The old man slapped the boy on the shoulder. "Help me get this bike down."

They each clasped a wheel, lifted the bike off the hooks, and lowered it to the ground.

The old man pointed to the door. "I want to take it into my workshop and give it an overhaul."

The boy gripped the bike by the seat and handlebars. "Let me carry it in for you. It's not too heavy for me."

"Thank you." The old man couldn't remember when age had humbled him. In his younger years his pride would prevent him from allowing anyone to help with simple tasks. Now he knew that kind of pride did not define the true person. He had discovered humility was a strength rather than a weakness.

The boy awkwardly managed to carry the bike up the steep back steps and onto the porch. The old man pulled the screen door open and held it so the boy could enter the kitchen. By now the boy was breathing heavily. He lowered the bike to the floor and leaned it against a small Formica-topped table. Two folding chairs sat at each end. On the wall next to the table hung a picture of Jesus, the one of him kneeling and praying on a large rock in the garden of Gethsemane. His late wife, a committed Methodist, had placed the picture there early in their marriage, and the old man had never taken it down out of memory for her and respect for those who suffer and endure. However, he did remove their thirtieth anniversary photograph taken at J.C. Penny's because it made him feel hollow inside. He kept it in a bottom drawer of her dresser beneath folded socks which had not been worn for ten years.

"How will this bike help you run the marathon?" the boy asked.

"Cross training," the old man said. "Now I run six to eight miles every day with no sciatica pain. Maybe if I ride the bike every other day instead of running, I could increase the length of my runs. Work my way up to twenty."

"That's a good plan."

6

"How would you like to see me run a marathon in three hours and thirty minutes and easily qualify for Boston?"

"Could you run it that fast?"

"I believe I could."

"Coach Silvers ran three thirty-four and he's at least ten years younger than you."

"He narrowly qualified for his age group."

"How do you know?"

The old man pointed to a stack of running magazines on the table. "I read. For someone his age he must run three thirty-five or better."

"How about someone your age?"

"I'm sixty-three. I would have to run under three hours and fifty-five minutes to qualify."

"If you ran three thirty, then you would beat the qualifying time by almost half an hour."

"That's right. The bike could be my answer."

The boy grasped the handlebars and seat and lifted the bike. "May I carry it to your workshop and clean it up for you?" The boy knew the old man worried about his lower back.

"Of course."

🏃🏃🏃🏃🏃

In the basement of the house, in a room with peg-board walls filled with tools, the boy worked under the glow of a fluorescent light that hung from a joist on two chains. With a bottle of window cleaner and paper towels he removed the dust from the bike frame. The handlebars had become pitted with rust and the seat covering had split, exposing foam, but the yellow-painted frame looked new with the dust removed.

"It's in pretty good shape," the boy said.

"A few adjustments. Some oil for the chain and gears. New tires and seat. Before long I'll have it looking new. On Monday I'll take it out for a long ride in the country, to Mount Pleasant or even Harrisville."

"Clear to Harrisville? That's a long way."

"It's a start. Thirty miles perhaps out and back."

The boy rubbed his backside. "That would be hard on the rear end."

"Yes. I'll try to find a comfortable seat at the bike shop but one that's not too wide."

The boy looked at his watch. "It's almost ten o'clock. Are you hungry?"

"A little."

"Do you have something to eat? I could bring you something from home later."

"I'm sure there's filet mignon or lobster tail in the refrigerator. I'll be fine."

The boy knew the old man was kidding. His refrigerator usually held a few items—eggs, apples, celery, and sometimes sliced turkey or ham. Often the boy's mother sent the old man leftovers.

"I must be going, but I'll be back about noon. Are you going to work on the bike?"

"Yes. I'll do what I can this morning, and later in the afternoon I'll go to the bike shop and get what I need."

"Do you want to know what I think, Angelo?"

The old man gazed at the boy, noticing the sincerity in his eyes. "Tell me what you think."

"Three hours and thirty minutes would be difficult for your first marathon, but I believe you can do it."

"Remember this, Manny. Courage requires choosing the difficult thing, taking chances, and making sacrifices. Never settle for what comes easy."

The boy nodded. "I'll remember that. I have to head home now, but I'll be back in a couple hours."

"See you then."

人人人人人

At noon the boy returned to find the old man asleep on his recliner, shirtless with a running magazine resting on his chest. In the glow of the reading light he noticed how strong the old man's shoulders, arms and chest appeared. It was an odd sight, the thin, tanned and blotched skin covering such well-defined muscles. His gray hair, thick and combed back, was in need of a trim. He wore cut-off gray sweat pants with splatters of white paint on them. Thick calluses rimmed the balls and heels of his feet, and both big toes had blackened toenails.

The boy went back into the kitchen to let the old man sleep. For about half an hour he thumbed through the running magazines the old man had piled on the table and read about the best training programs to set a personal record in a 5K. He then placed a container he had brought with him in the microwave and set it to four minutes. After he placed two plates and silverware on the table, he returned to the living room. The old man seemed frozen in the same position, his face peaceful, his chest slowly rising and falling.

The boy put his hand on the old man's shoulder. "Wake up, Angelo."

The old man opened his eyes, but his expression gave the impression he was lingering on some faraway shore. Then he smiled, and the boy knew he had stepped out of his dream world.

"You're back," the old man said.

"And I've brought us some lunch."

"I'm not too hungry."

"If you're going to train for the marathon, you need to eat."

The old man sat up, the magazine falling into his lap. He retracted the footrest of his recliner. "What have you got?"

"Lasagna, left over from last night's supper."

"Ahhh. I can eat your mother's lasagna even when I'm not hungry."

"What were you reading about?"

9

The old man lifted the magazine. On the front was a picture of Bill Rodgers crossing the finish line at the New York City Marathon. "An article about the top ten American marathoners of all time."

"Come out to the kitchen table and you can tell me about America's great marathoners."

They entered the kitchen and the boy took the container from the microwave. The old man sat at the table and picked up his knife and fork while the boy dished out the lasagna.

"I must remember to thank your mother next time I see her," the old man said.

"I already thanked her. There's no need for you to thank her again."

"She feeds me often. I'll thank her and give her a dozen tomatoes from my garden."

"She does like tomatoes."

"I'll send them with you."

"Would you like a beer with your lasagna?"

"Yes, and get yourself a soda."

The boy placed the container into the sink and got their drinks from the refrigerator.

After he sat down the old man said, "Are you ready to eat?"

"I've been ready. You're the one who's been sleeping like a worn out greyhound."

The old man cut a large chunk from the thick slab of noodles and sauce and forked it into his mouth. "Your mother's lasagna is excellent."

"Tell me about the great American marathoners," the boy said.

"Most of them are from the old days when I was in my prime," the old man said happily.

"Not so many great ones today, huh?"

"Today the Kenyans and Ethiopians are great. In the seventies and eighties the Americans were great."

"Are you talking about the days of Bill Rodgers and Frank Shorter?" the boy asked.

"Of course. Dick Beardlsy, Amby Burfoot, Craig Virgin, and Alberto Salazar."

"Who was the best?"

"All of them were good. Shorter won gold in the '72 and '76 Olympics, and Rodgers won New York and Boston four times each, but none compared with the Great One."

"The Great One? Who was he?"

"Johnny Kelley. He won the Boston Marathon twice . . ."

"What's so great about that? You just said Rodgers won four times."

The old man held up his hand. "Let me finish, young one. Kelley won the Boston twice, but he ran it sixty-one times."

"That's not possible is it?"

The old man nodded. "That's why he is known as the Great One, the Runner of the Century. He ran his last Boston in 1992 at the age of eighty-four. To me, he's an inspiration."

"Did you ever meet any of these great marathoners?"

"Yes. I met Bill Rodgers on several occasions. He ran the Elby's 20K in Wheeling many times. I liked him because he didn't put on airs. Many elite runners are arrogant. Not Rodgers. He enjoyed talking with us common runners. He would even warm up with us."

"I wonder how good Bill Rodgers was when he was my age?"

The old man shrugged. "I don't know. When I was your age I went on my first distance run. My father took me hunting and fishing on the Outer Banks, and I went for a run along the seashore with the wild horses."

"I know. You have told me that story."

"Shall we talk about the Outer Banks or marathons?"

"Marathons, I think," the boy said. "Tell me more about the Great One, Johnny Kelley."

"The Great One may have only won Boston twice, but he finished second seven times and in the top five fifteen times. No one has ever come close to matching that. To me, a great distance runner endures for many years and races until he is a very old man."

"Like you?" the boy asked.

"No. I am not so great. I could name many others who are better."

"But not around here. You are the best old runner in the Ohio Valley."

The old man lifted his hands and hunched his shoulders. "Maybe."

"There are many good young runners and a few great ones, but there is only one you."

"Thank you." The old man patted his chest. "Your words make me happy, but I hope the marathon doesn't prove you wrong. It may be too great a challenge for me."

"No marathon will defeat you. You may be old, but you're very strong."

"Maybe not as strong as you think," the old man said. "But I know some new tricks, and I have great determination. I've learned how to stretch properly and the importance of massage. I think the bike will be the key. It will help me do the necessary training without re-aggravating my sciatica."

The boy glanced at his watch. "I told my mother I'd be home by 1:30 to do my chores. What time are you running your intervals in the morning?"

"Early. Seven a.m."

"Will you stop by and get me? Just blow your horn. It will be my alarm clock."

"I don't need an alarm clock. Age is mine. I will come by and beep twice. Don't make me wait too long or I'll leave you behind."

"One minute is all I need. I sleep in my running shorts. My shoes are by my bed and my t-shirt is hanging on the doorknob. Time me. I'll be in your car in one minute or less."

The old man raised his wrist and tapped his watch. "I'll time you, and then you'll time me."

"That's a deal," the boy said. "I'll be your coach, but you'll find out I expect your best."

"That's okay with me. I don't mind hard work."

"Then you better sleep well tonight."

The old man smiled, thinking the boy's company might motivate him to run the intervals harder. "Wait here. I'll get those tomatoes for your mother."

🏃🏃🏃🏃

After the boy left, the old man drove to the bike shop in Aetnaville and purchased a cushioned seat, new brake pads, two new tires and inner tubes. When he arrived home, he brewed a pot of coffee and spent the afternoon and part of the evening upgrading and adjusting the bike. By the time he finished, it looked almost new. He even managed to remove most of the rust from the handlebars and rims. Cautiously, he lifted it, carried it up the basement steps into the kitchen and out the back door. He leaned the bike against the porch railing and stretched his back. Feeling no pain or numbness in his leg, he carried it down the steps and into the back yard.

There he mounted the bike and pedaled along the sidewalk at the side of the house and onto First Street. He picked up speed as he headed north past the high school football stadium, clicking through all the gears to make sure they shifted properly, taking mental note of any further adjustments to be made. It feels good to be on a racing bike again, he thought, as he sailed past the city garages, marina, and community baseball field. He turned around at the end of First Street in front of the steel mill where he had toiled for thirty-five years. The red building, covered with corrugated metal sheeting, loomed above him as if it threatened to draw him back into its dismal interior and force him to labor at the mouth of a fiery furnace. The odd sensation sent a shot of adrenaline through him, causing his legs to pump the pedals with fury. He flew past the stock yards, coal piles, and smoke stacks to where the railroad tracks

13

crossed the road and ran along the top of the bank near the river. From there he coasted for several hundred yards. The bike gave him a sense of speed and freedom and escape.

The sun had set, and twilight descended, draining away the colors of the day. By the time the old man reached home he felt tired but good. He dismounted the bike and walked it to the back of the house and into the garage. He'd showered earlier in the day and didn't believe a four mile bike ride warranted another dousing. Tomorrow after the half-mile intervals he would soak himself in a bathtub full of cool water. He entered the house and climbed the steps to the second floor. In his bedroom he tossed his clothes into a basket near the closet door, crawled onto the bed, and wrapped himself in a sheet. He reached for the remote and powered on the television. John Wayne on horseback appeared on the screen in black and white. This was his favorite channel—classic movies.

He fell asleep to the sounds of hoofs pattering along western trails. He dreamed of the Outer Banks when he was a boy running on the wide, beautiful beaches dotted with many fine shells left behind by the receding tide. The high dunes with their sea oats waving in the breeze rose up on his left and the blue-green ocean roared on his right as its waves rolled and crashed, sending water and foam rushing up the bank. Ahead he saw the ribs of an old shipwreck lying on the ground like the bones of a dinosaur, recently unveiled by the relentless wind and shifting sands. He slowed to a stop and stood among the timbers of the ancient ship.

Its remains had endured for hundreds of years, perhaps since the 1600s. He pondered how everything is born and then grows old and dies. You can't beat death, he thought, but you can endure with determination to the end. Ahead, at the top of the dunes, he saw a black horse descending the sand hill followed by a gray mare and two spotted colts. They crossed the beach and frolicked in the waves. He ran in their direction, and when he passed them, they joined him. Together, the old man and the horse family trotted down the beach.

This was his favorite dream. Sleep transported him to this beach almost every night. When he ran with the horses, he felt like a young boy who could hold a fast pace for miles without the aches and pains of age. He no longer dreamed of labor or women or accomplishments or conflicts or road races or his wife. He dreamed only of the Outer Banks and the horses on the beach. They pranced through the waves and tossed their manes with exultation, and he loved them like he loved the boy, but he never dreamed about the boy.

When he awoke, the sun was peaking over the Appalachian foothills, shining its rays across the river and through his bedroom window. He rose slowly, stretching, knowing his muscles, joints, and bones needed time to loosen and warm before he would feel comfortable. He walked to the bathroom, urinated an unsteady stream, and flushed the toilet. When he washed his face, he noticed the large bags under his eyes and deep wrinkles across his forehead and cheeks. But his eyes were wide and bright, and today he would challenge himself by running eight half-mile intervals at a 3:15 pace or better.

By the time he shaved, dressed, and laced up his running shoes it was almost seven, and the sun had risen above the hills, setting the boughs of the maples, birches, and oaks along the river aglow. He pulled his old Dodge out of the garage, drove two blocks to the boy's house and parked along the curb. After beeping his horn twice, he started his stopwatch. Two minutes later the boy rushed out the front door, funneling into a blue t-shirt.

"What's the matter?" the old man asked. "Too early for you?"

"No way. I'm ready to go." The boy swung open the rusted door and climbed in the car.

The old man drove down First Street, turned up Hanover Street, and stopped at the red light at the Route 7 intersection.

"Are we stopping for coffee?" the boy asked.

The old man nodded. "I see the golden arches up ahead. Are you buying?"

"I didn't bring money."

"You never bring money."

The boy slid open the ash tray on the dash. "I just found two dollar bills."

The light turned green, and the old man drove across the intersection, up the hill, and turned right into a McDonald's. At the speaker he ordered two coffees with cream and then pulled to the pickup window. A smiling, round-faced woman with thinning brown hair handed the old man the coffees and told him to have a nice day.

"Thank you," he said and handed the boy one of the cups.

The boy sipped from the hole in the lid. "My mother says I've begun a bad habit. Is drinking coffee that bad for you?"

"I must respectfully disagree with your mother. I've read that coffee prevents cancer and diabetes. It's good for your brain too, keeps you from getting Alzheimer's disease. Best of all it increases endurance in distance runners and bikers."

"Is that why you drink so much?"

"No."

The old man smiled. "If I don't drink it, I get headaches."

"Doesn't it keep you up at nights?"

"Not at all. It puts me to sleep."

"How did you sleep last night?"

"Very well, Manny. I feel confident I'll hit my pace on these intervals."

"With me coaching you, so do I."

🏃🏃🏃🏃🏃

The high school track was located on top of a hill above the town, built on land formerly used to quarry limestone. If one stood in the eighth lane on the east turn and gazed into the valley, he could see the Ohio River far below and perhaps a barge full of coal chugging toward Wheeling Island. No other facility around matched the spectacular view.

As the car slowed to a stop near the chain link fence, the old man noticed a runner jogging on the backstretch. The man was of medium height and weight with dark brown hair. He wore a purple tank top and bright white running shoes that flashed in the morning sunshine.

"That's Coach Silvers," the boy said. "He's training for his next race."

"A marathon?"

"Maybe."

They exited the vehicle, walked through the gate, and stood on the track. The old man bent down to touch his toes. He heard footsteps approaching and glanced up. Coach Silvers slowed to a stop in front of them. He had a thick brown mustache and intense dark eyes.

"Good morning, Emmanuel," Silvers said. "Come to do some track work?"

"No sir. Just timing. This is my friend, Angelo."

The old man held out his hand and the coach shook it firmly, and said, "Jack Silvers."

"Nice to meet you. I've heard you are a good marathoner."

"I do okay. Ran Boston a few times. Are you a marathoner?"

"No. Not yet."

"But he will be," the boy said.

"I see. First time you've ever trained for one?"

"No. I've had bad luck. Twenty years ago I trained for one but ended up injured."

"Hoping for better luck this time, huh?"

"I hope so."

"Angelo is fast for his age," the boy said. "I have no doubt he'll run a great marathon and qualify for Boston."

"Emmanuel believes in you."

The old man tousled the boy's hair. "He has great confidence in me, but the marathon doesn't show favoritism."

"Or mercy," Jack Silvers said.

The old man nodded, thinking Silvers seemed self-assured.

"Are you running intervals today too?" the boy asked.

17

"Yes. Six one milers under seven minutes a mile. It's a good speed workout for the marathon." Silvers eyed the old man. "Would you like to join me?"

The old man usually didn't adjust his training schedule to accommodate someone else, but Silvers' offer seemed like a challenge. The boy had told him his coach had run a three thirty-four marathon, and he reasoned he could run at least that fast. Running against Silvers would be a good test. "I'll try it. Can't promise I'll keep up with you, though."

"You've got a few years on me. Don't worry about keeping up. Just do your best."

"I'll time both of you," the boy said.

After completing four warm-up laps and stretching, the two men toed the starting line, Silvers in the first lane and the old man in the second. The boy sat on the wooden timer steps with his finger poised on his watch's start button. "Ready. Go!"

For the first two laps the old man hung just off Silvers' shoulder around the turns but pulled even on the straight-a-ways. The pace seemed fast, 3:23 at the half-mile. Silvers pushed the pace on the next two laps, and the old man slipped into the first lane and ran a few yards behind. They finished in 6:44 and 6:47 respectively—a good effort for the first one, more than ten seconds ahead of goal pace.

The second and third interval mirrored the first, but the old man noticed that Silvers' breathing had become labored during the last lap of the third one. The coach leaned on his knees for a full minute sucking in air. This filled the old man with confidence as they approached the line for the fourth interval. The boy yelled, "Go!" and they took off. Silvers remained strong for the first lap. The old man took the lead on the second lap but could hear Silvers' footfalls not far behind. On the last lap Silvers pulled even as they crossed the finish line. The effort took its toll on the coach. Silvers stepped over the curb and dropped into the grass on his hands and knees.

The rest between the fourth and fifth interval was too long, but Silvers wouldn't come directly to the line when the boy announced their three minutes were up. He said he needed a drink and spent at least two minutes walking to the fountain and back. By the time Silvers came to the starting line, the old man felt fully recovered, which really did not please him because one should feel quite stressed at this point in the workout.

The boy shouted, "Go!" and they took off. The old man took the lead from the start. Silvers' breathing became strained even before they finished the first lap. The old man decided to push the pace. It wasn't long before he couldn't hear Silvers' footsteps or breathing. He finished in 6:35, almost a half a lap ahead of Silvers. The coach crossed the line with a pained expression, favoring his right leg.

"My hamstring is tightening up on me," Silvers said. "Happens every once in a while."

"Sorry to hear that," the old man said. He really had no pity on Silvers but he tried not to show it. "Maybe you'll feel better on the last one."

"Maybe," Silvers said.

After the three minute rest interval the boy called them to the line.

"I better let you go it alone," Silvers said, rubbing his right hamstring. "I don't want to take the chance of tearing this thing."

"I don't blame you," the old man said. "Hamstrings take a while to heal."

The boy set him off on the last interval, and the old man ran the first lap aggressively. When he heard his lap time, 1:30, he smiled, although he knew the pace was much too fast. He tried to relax every muscle in his body and maintain a fluid stride. He hit the half mile in 3:07 and noticed Jack Silvers eyeing him as he flew by. By the third lap he was breathing hard but wanted to show the boy his toughness in front of his coach. He ran the last lap all out and would not allow himself to crumple into the grass but instead crossed the line and kept walking, breathing hard but in control.

"That was your fastest one—6:22!" the boy shouted.

The old man turned around and walked back to them.

"Nice effort," the coach said. "How old are you?"

"Sixty-three." The old man could tell Silvers was impressed but embarrassed by his own collapse. The old man didn't want to say anything else to further humiliate him. "I hope your hamstring heals quickly."

"I'll be fine," the coach said. "I wish you luck in training for the marathon."

"Thank you. I'll need it."

"What kind of injury did you have when you attempted to train for your first one?"

"Sciatica."

The coach rubbed his chin. "How bad?"

"Pretty bad. I lost total feeling in my leg and couldn't run for eight years afterwards."

"Sorry to hear that. To be honest with you, I wouldn't recommend that you attempt the marathon."

"He'll be fine," the boy said. "He has a lot of experience now."

"I plan on cross training," the old man said.

The coach shook his head. "I had a friend who had the same goal as you—to run a marathon after severe sciatica problems."

"Did he make it?" the boy asked.

"He made it to mile twenty-four but then lost all feeling in his right leg. He couldn't finish. The nerves were badly damaged. Now he's partially paralyzed and walks with a cane. If I were you, I'd stick with 5Ks."

But you're not me, the old man thought, but he didn't say anything, only smiled and nodded.

𝆬𝆬𝆬𝆬𝆬

The next morning long before sunrise, the old man awoke, dressed quickly, and descended the steps to the kitchen. He put a pot of coffee on to brew while he washed his face, shaved, and relieved himself. He looked forward to his first long bike ride in twelve years. It felt like an adventure, a new path that may lead to his

20

first successful marathon. For breakfast he ate toasted waffles with a banana sliced over them and plenty of syrup, a meal that would not weigh heavy on his stomach. After washing them down with coffee, he poured another cup to drink as he sat on his back porch.

This was the time of day he missed his wife the most. In the old days they would always drink coffee together before he left for work. As he savored the bitter liquid, he could sense her presence next to him. In her younger years she had long blonde hair and a fine lean body. When she entered her forties, she decided a shorter hairstyle was more appropriate as her hips became wider and her breasts bigger. He did not mind the physical changes age wrought because he loved who she was on the inside. But whenever he sat on the back porch in the morning and drank coffee, he always pictured her younger appearance, the slim body and long hair.

The wind blew from the north with a slight chill, bringing with it the harsh smell of sulfur and the haze of smoke from the steel mill's tall stacks. The odor didn't bother him as much as the memory it engendered of long hours under harsh and confined conditions. As he pushed the bike out of the garage, he decided to do a long ride into the country. Because he was in good shape from running, he knew a twenty-five mile ride wouldn't bother him much, except for maybe his rear end.

He pushed the bike to the street, straddled it, and launched himself, quickly picking up speed to where the gears offered the right resistance, just enough stress to raise oxygen demand. He didn't believe in riding leisurely. For cross training to be effective, it had to be demanding. The fastest way into the country would be to take the Colerain Pike so he turned up Center Street past the meat packing plant, the Liberty Fire Station, and the old elementary school. The six hundred yard uphill stretch was a good warm up for the mile-and-a-half climb to the top of the pike. By the time he turned down Zane Highway he was breathing hard but feeling good. He glided down a slight grade for about a half mile and turned right onto Route 647 which led up the long and winding road.

The hill began immediately. Fortunately, the pollution of First Street had dissipated this far from the river; he took a deep breath, thankful the air didn't have that toxic tinge to it. Halfway up, his legs tired and his breathing grew labored. He didn't mind. Good training was like life—never easy and often uphill. He lowered his head and focused on the rhythm of pumping the pedals. Get used to it, he told himself. Many more hills awaited on the journey.

Down the other side he flew, pedaling as fast as he could in high gear. He didn't have a speedometer but guessed he approached thirty-five miles per hour. The wind whipped his tank top and rustled his hair, quickly drying the sweat that had begun to drip down his forehead and ribcage. He leaned around a severe turn, overcome with that precarious feeling of maintaining his balance under the stress of centrifugal force. At the bottom of the hill he kept pedaling in high gear for as long as he could.

When he came to a "Y" in the road he veered right toward Mount Pleasant, up another challenging hill. It didn't take long for the grade to force him into a much lower gear. To get his mind off the strain of the climb, he listened to the birds. The air was fresh and clean this far out, and their songs added a vitality to the atmosphere. He saw small brown sparrows, bright red cardinals, and blue jays. He detected the high tweet of finches, the pleasant warble of orioles, and the low cooing of morning doves. Ahead he heard the ugly cawing of crows, and when he rounded a turn, he saw their black shape shifting above the bloody remains of an unfortunate raccoon. They pecked and tore at the carcass until he came upon them and shouted, "Git!" Then they scattered in different directions, as if one dark entity splintered into five ragged shapes.

By the time he reached the top of the hill, sweat poured into his eyes. He blinked, and with his fingers, swiped the burning liquid away. Now he would sail along the ridge for several miles, challenging the slight rises and falls of the road without having to preserve energy for a long uphill. The sun broke through overhanging limbs spattering the shadowed asphalt with bright splashes of light. There was great beauty in training. To most people a hard workout took on masculine qualities, but the old man felt training was feminine, like a lovely woman. Sometimes he praised her because of the surrounding magnificence of creation and the strength she gave him. At other times he cursed her because of the pain and injury she brought his way. Like a lover, she offered wonderful pleasures but at times withdrew them, leaving him longing and frustrated.

Of course, he also viewed training as a science. He kept up on all the latest articles and tried to apply the good advice and sound theories to his daily regimen. Some runners just went out and ran distance every day, not concerning themselves with technicalities. He wanted to do it right, to be exact in his application and balance of various workouts—speed training, tempo runs, fartlek, distance, and all the combinations. He also studied running injuries and learned how to prevent and overcome them. Through the years he'd faced most of the common problems—plantar fasciitis, runner's knee, Achilles tendonitis, hamstring and quad pulls, shin splints, stress fractures, and worst of all, sciatica. He had long since passed his prime, but at least now he knew when an injury was coming on and what to do. If he'd only known back then, he could have prevented many problems. By now he would have run several marathons. Oh well, my time may come yet, he thought.

After a long downhill, he began the two mile slight upgrade that led into the village of Mount Pleasant. This stretch was the most scenic of the ride with large oaks and maples overhanging the road casting their shifting shadows across the asphalt. To the right a brook babbled, its occasional small waterfalls pouring and splashing onto broken rocks and washing down the worn creek bed. Very little traffic and the sounds of nature heightened the sense of peace he felt along this section of road. It reminded him of the awe he had experienced as a child whenever he entered the sanctuary of the Grace Presbyterian Church and noticed the colored light rays cascading through the tall stained glass windows. To the old man, the outdoors was God's natural cathedral, far superior to anything manmade.

About a mile from Mount Pleasant he saw three bikers a few hundred yards ahead of him. He made it a goal to catch them before he reached the village. They were going at a decent pace, but not what he considered strenuous. Their white helmets flashed when they passed from the shadows into the sunshine. The old man never wore a helmet when he rode. He preferred an olive ball cap, one he had won for taking first in the grandmasters division at the Debbie Green 5k for Leukemia. His wife had always nagged him about wearing a helmet. She was a worrier. Back then it irked him, but now he missed her complaining.

He lowered his head and upped his effort, trying to keep his breathing under control and rhythmic. About one hundred yards before the "Welcome to Mount Pleasant" sign he drew near them, two young men and a woman, probably in their thirties. He could hear their voices and laughter but couldn't make out their words.

As silently as possible he drifted to the middle of the road to pass and said, "Good morning".

The girl gasped with surprise.

"Sorry. I didn't mean to frighten you."

"She scares easily," the man in front said.

"Beautiful day, huh?" the other man said.

"Gorgeous."

It didn't take long to pull away, but before the old man got out of earshot he heard the girl say, "He's twice our age and leaving us in his dust."

"Maybe three times our age," one of the men said.

Some athletes would be insulted by these words but not the old man. It made him chuckle. He may be old, but many younger people couldn't keep up with him. The words validated his victory over time and the ravages of age. It bolstered his belief in himself and the challenge of enduring to the end of life at the highest levels of fitness he could possibly maintain. This determination to endure had become his mantra. The effort to pull away made him breathe rapidly, but he picked up his pace anyway.

The village of Mount Pleasant was very historic with old brick homes and churches. Slate and brick sidewalks, buckled by the roots of large trees, lined the main street on both sides. The town had deep Quaker roots and was a bastion against slavery during the Civil War. Known for being a station on the Underground Railroad, the village prided itself in its longstanding support for human rights. It was a good place with fine people. So many towns and villages in the Ohio Valley had deteriorated due to difficult economic times and the temptation to reestablish a financial base through the gambling industry. Their caving in had served only to disgrace the once self-respecting communities. Riding through Mount Pleasant was a step back into time, a welcomed reprieve.

A mile beyond the village he passed the Seceder Cemetery, one of the oldest in the state. Hundreds of local pioneers were buried there, men and women who were the first to plant and plow this land in the early 1800s. He wondered if any were his relatives.

Now he prepared himself for a series of rolling hills with cow pastures and corn fields and woods along the sides of the road. These quick ups and downs tested his shifting skills. He tried to build great speed by the time he reached the bottom and then maintain the higher gears up the next hill until the resistance forced him back into lower gears.

He pedaled furiously down the third hill. At the bottom a deer shot through a farmer's field and across the road. The old man jerked his handbrakes, skidding to a stop, missing the large doe by inches. "You damn whore!" It kicked its hind legs up before springing into the woods, its tail flashing white. His heart rattled in his chest, and his scalp felt electrified. Now he had to somehow get the bike into low gear from a dead stop to climb the hill. This wasn't easy, but he managed, almost losing his balance as the chain slipped and caught unevenly in the process. He'd known a motorcyclist and bicyclist who'd run into deer. The biker ended up with a broken a leg, but the motorcyclist had flipped over a large buck and landed on his head, killing him instantly because he wasn't wearing a helmet.

The old man's wife's warning echoed in the back of his mind: *You better wear that helmet before you end up dead too.*

"Don't worry about me, woman," he said. "When my time comes, it comes." He often spoke aloud to his wife, even though he knew she was long gone. Was it a sign of mental instability? No, he told himself, just a sign of loneliness.

After a few more rolling hills he turned left onto State Route 250, thirteen or so miles into the journey. His butt ached, so he stood and pedaled up the next hill. Maybe twenty-five miles for his first ride in years wasn't so wise. At the top he pulled off in front of Alisha's Country Restaurant. He had twelve miles to go and needed a butt break. A cup of coffee and a Danish sounded good. The establishment looked more like a house converted into a restaurant. It had white siding with a small sign hanging above the entry. The old man had eaten here a few times and enjoyed the good country cooking.

He entered and seated himself at a small table for two. Smiling widely, a thin lady maybe fifty years old, approached with a menu. She had bright teeth, short dark hair, and thick black eyelashes— quite a beauty. Thinking she had a fit look to her, he glanced at her left hand and didn't notice a wedding ring. He had no great goal to pursue a relationship at this point in life but didn't mind keeping the possibility alive.

"Good morning, sir," she said, placing the menu in front of him.

He waved his hand. "No need for that. I know what I want."

"A man who knows his own mind. I like that." She winked at him.

"You always wink at strange men?"

"Just the good-looking ones." She touched his shoulder and laughed. "What'll you have, handsome?"

"Cup of coffee and a Danish."

"Cherry, all right?"

He nodded. "Could you zap it in the microwave?"

"Sure. Hot coffee and a hot Danish coming up." She winked again.

"Not too hot, young lady. I don't want to burn my tongue."

She patted his cheek. "Anyone who calls me 'young lady' gets his Danish exactly how he wants it."

She walked away with a wiggle, and he chuckled to himself. It would be nice to have a woman again. But that was something to weigh carefully; he enjoyed his independence. He did what he wanted to do when he wanted to do it. Perhaps he had become too used to living his own way. Besides, she was at least ten years younger than he and incredibly good looking. She was out of his league.

It felt good to sit on a chair that supported his entire rear end. He took his time drinking the coffee and eating the Danish. The waitress came often to refill his cup. He sensed she wanted him to make a pass, but he didn't, although he behaved very cordially to her. As he popped the last piece of Danish into his mouth, he saw several people entering the restaurant. They were removing white helmets, and he recognized them—the bikers he had passed before entering Mount Pleasant.

When he made eye contact with them, he noticed the hint of recognition in their expressions. They walked in his direction and sat at the table next to him.

"Decided to stop for a break too?" one of the men asked.

"Yes," the old man said. "This is my first ride in quite a few years. I'm not used to sitting so long on a narrow seat. Needed to get the blood flowing down there again."

The trio laughed and agreed with him. Then the pony tailed blonde girl asked, "How do you ride so fast, if this is your first time out in years?"

"I run every day, but now I've decided to cross train to preserve my body for longer runs. I hope to train for a marathon."

The girl said, "A marathon! I'm impressed. I could never run that far."

One of the men, a redhead with blondish stubble across his jowls said, "I'd think twice about that if I were you. Recently several people died running marathons in Chicago and New York."

"That wouldn't be a bad way to die," the old man said.

The thin waitress, her bright teeth flashing, approached his table. "Is that how you want to die?" She asked. "Running a marathon?"

"That would be fine with me, but that's not how I *want* to die."

"Don't tell me," the waitress said. She slipped her hand onto his shoulder, her thigh brushing his elbow. "You want to die in the arms of a beautiful woman while making passionate love."

The young people laughed loudly.

The old man felt his cheeks burning red but could not keep a smile from breaking across his face. "That would be a fine way to go, but . . ."

The waitress stood straight, jamming her hands against her hips. "But what?"

"But to die running would be my preference. Years from now, when I'm ninety or so, I'd like to go out for a long run in the country. On some remote dirt road my heart gives out. Hopefully, I'll have enough strength to crawl into the woods where no one could find me. There in the beautiful surroundings of nature I'd decompose, becoming a part of God's green earth again. Dust to dust."

The waitress threw back her head, cackled, and then eyed him. "Are you serious?"

The old man nodded.

"But what about your family? They would wonder what happened to you."

He shrugged. "I'm a widower with no kids. Thirty years from now not too many people will notice I'm missing."

The waitress raised her eyebrows. "A single man, huh? Let me see your palm."

The old man held up his hand. "Do you read fortunes?"

"Yes." With one hand she supported the back of his hand and with the other she took her pen and wrote something on his palm. Then she folded his hand closed. "This information will be very important to your future."

The old man opened his hand to see a name and number. He was surprised at her boldness. Was she just trying to be funny? He glanced at the young people and noticed wide smiles on all of their faces. Perhaps this was a joke. He focused on her eyes. They were big and brown with long lashes.

Thank you, Miss . . ." He glanced at his palm again, ". . . Miss Rita Marling." He held up his hand. "Is this the next winning Powerball number?"

"No. But you'll need that number if you want to catch me."

The old man nodded and stood. "Okay. I'll be dropping you a line."

"Soon, I hope." She winked and walked across the room to wait on other customers.

The old man pulled a five dollar bill from the pocket of his athletic shorts, dropped it on the table for the tip, picked up his bill and headed to the cash register near the entrance. He nodded at the young people as he passed their table. The blonde girl wished him good luck. He thanked her, wondering if she meant good luck in running the marathon or in wooing the waitress.

All the way home he kept thinking about Rita Marling. Was that her real name or was she playing some kind of game? The sun, now higher in the sky, beat down on him, and he swiped sweat from his forehead. As he pumped up the hills he focused on getting the bike into the right gear. On the down hills, though, he coasted and replayed the scene in the restaurant—the tone of Rita Marling's voice, the touch of her hand, and the depths of those dark brown eyes. Should he call her that evening? No. That would appear too anxious. He'd wait a couple of days. Perhaps this was a bad idea. A relationship with a woman may prove detrimental to his new training goals. As he sailed down the final winding hill into Martins Ferry, he felt greatly conflicted.

He coasted into his driveway, feeling weary, his butt sore and throat dry. But despite the effects of the long ride, his spirit soared. The beautiful Miss Marling waited to be caught. Was she really attracted to him? Why not? He was old and wrinkled but not wretched. He had a good body for his age, thin and muscular. Hopefully, she wasn't interested in his money. He lived on a steelworker's pension in a humble abode down by the river. Perhaps she would be greatly disappointed at his station in life. How could she be, though? Obviously she wasn't one of the Rockefellers, only a waitress at a country restaurant. Maybe they would make a good pair.

He rolled the bike into the garage and leaned it against the wall. Glancing at his palm, he could not see her name or number due to the lack of light. He hurried outside and held his hand in the sunlight. The ink had been smeared to unrecognizable scribbles because of his sweaty palms on the handle grips. *Dammit!* He peered into the sky. Was this a sign from God? The sun, peeking from behind a wispy cloud, made him squint. Although he did not consider himself religious, he did feel a spiritual connection with God, especially when he ran along a country road ablaze with the colors of fall trees or over a blanket of virgin snow. Despite his limited biblical knowledge, he believed he knew God's character: the Almighty was like a good distance runner, one who understood commitment and sacrifice. Sometimes odd things happened that made him think twice. The smeared ink alerted him to the possibility of God's warning: Pursuing a relationship with this woman might be a distraction during the next eight months as he prepared for the race.

He headed up the steps to the back door. Rita Marling's face, those big brown eyes and the white flash of her teeth, reflected in the pool of his memory. He shook his head to clear the image, but it only rippled like when a pebble breaks the surface of a pond. This would not be easy—forgetting Rita Marling. It had been a long time since he had felt the kind of urges she had stirred within him. At the restaurant he had told her that he would drop her a line. He was a man of his word. Now he didn't know what to do. Maybe he could look up her number in the phone book.

In the kitchen he eyed the picture of Jesus kneeling at the rock in the Garden of Gethsemane. Christ never pursued a woman. His face was set like flint toward the cross and suffering. The marathon was a difficult challenge, especially for a runner with a history of sciatica. If he compromised his focus, would God honor his effort? At least he needed to inform Rita Marling of his circumstances. Maybe they were only meant to be friends. He decided that on his next bike ride he would stop by the restaurant again to see her. Hopefully, she would understand the level of his commitment in preparation for a marathon and not expect him to focus on her.

The next morning the old man went for a ten-mile run across the Aetnaville Bridge onto Wheeling Island and then over the Wheeling Suspension Bridge to the asphalt trail along the river. It was the longest distance he had attempted in years. Usually he limited himself to eight miles out of fear he would aggravate the sciatica nerve, but his new training plan gave him courage to extend the distance. Tomorrow he would bike again out to Alisha's Country Restaurant. Then he would run again in two days. This was the key—alternating running and biking.

As he trotted along, he pictured Rita Marling on the screen of his mind. He could not clearly remember her face, only those big brown eyes and flash of white teeth. Growing old frustrated him— the loss of mental acuity, forgetting where he put things, difficulty with recalling names. But he pressed on, battling against the mounting years. While most other men his age sat around the house watching television, maybe getting some exercise at the bowling alley or on the golf course, he logged hundreds of miles a year on the roads. He believed it kept his body ten years younger or even twenty. But it did not help his mind. Now he longed to see Rita again to capture the image of her face and try to burn it into his memory. Why did he feel so tickled like a lovesick school boy? How easily a pretty woman could commandeer a man's thoughts.

To take his mind off Rita, he glanced to his left at the Ohio River. Just beyond the asphalt path the bank steeply descended to the water. A great barge with several sections full of coal chugged along just ahead of him. He was catching up to it. He may be old but could run faster than a barge. He estimated the vessel's speed to be about five miles an hour. His mental speedometer was fairly accurate: his pace—about seven miles an hour. With every step he crept ahead of the big barge. He was running north along the river. The barge was heading against the flow of the river in the direction of Pittsburgh about sixty-five miles away. Pittsburgh! Of course. The Pittsburgh Marathon would be the right choice. The race was held in early May. That would give him seven months to prepare. Then he could run Boston in April of the following year, that is if he qualified.

The old man soon reached the five-mile turnaround spot—a deer crossing sign along Route 2 near Warwood, West Virginia. All the way home he thought about racing at Pittsburgh. The course would have hills but he was a strength runner. His strong arms and muscular legs gave him an advantage on the hills. Besides, Boston had hills. The Steel City wasn't too far away—an hour and twenty minutes if the traffic wasn't bad. He could drive up the day before and pick up his packet if need be. Perhaps he would stay in a hotel. He wondered if Rita would like to accompany him. Get your mind off that woman, he scolded himself.

🏃🏃🏃🏃🏃

The days and weeks and months of training passed. In November when high school cross country season ended, the boy ran with him again. Emmanuel's parents did not complain much. Coach Silvers' winter conditioning program started in January. Until then, they figured it would not hurt for the boy to train with the old man. The boy was getting stronger and had no problem running the longer distances—ten and twelve milers. As a freshman he had become one of the top three runners on the team. The old man was very proud of him. He loved the boy very much and wanted to see him excel and one day become a champion. He treasured the days the boy ran with him because the boy gave him life. Perhaps his youth and enthusiasm rubbed off on the old man. In the boy's presence, he realized every day was a gift and every step a blessing. Tomorrow was not guaranteed. His running career could end at a moment's notice—a pinched nerve, a torn tendon, a bout with cancer. At his age too many things could go wrong. Each day that passed he celebrated the gift of running, thinking that if tomorrow came and with it another opportunity to train, he would celebrate again.

On Sundays the old man did his long run. He believed this workout was extremely important to marathon success. It toughened the body and the mind. For the body the long run conditioned the muscles to help delay the onset of fatigue. Perhaps the greater benefit, though, was bestowed upon the mind. Covering all those miles increased self-confidence and produced a positive mental outlook. In September he had started at thirteen miles, but every three weeks he would add a mile. By the end of November he was up to seventeen miles. The boy's parents limited Manny to twelve miles. That was fine with the old man. They would run a twelve-mile loop into the country and back where he would drop Manny off and then head out for four more miles on his own. When he finished he felt incredibly tired but hopeful. As he completed each Sunday long run, he knew 26.2 miles was not out of his range.

The old man stuck to his regimen, alternating running and biking days. When he rode out to Mount Pleasant, he often stopped at Alisha's Restaurant to spend time with Rita Marling. She always greeted him warmly and flirted with him. His confidence grew with each visit until he got up the nerve to ask her out to dinner, but she claimed to have another engagement. This threw the old man off. Had he misjudged Rita Marling? At their first encounter she had seemed to like him a lot. Had she changed her mind now that she knew him better? Maybe she was playing hard to get. Perhaps she acted this way with every lonely old man that walked into the restaurant. He decided not to give up on the possibility of romancing her. Long distance running had taught him patience and persistence. When the time was right, he would try again.

By December the weather had become too cold to bike. The old man made a trip out to Sears at the Ohio Valley Mall to pick up a good stationary bike. He settled on a Nordic Track model with a recumbent design and magnetic resistance for around $650. He took the money out of his savings account because he refused to charge anything. Besides, he rarely spent money on any extravagance. He had earned his pension the hard way—backbreaking labor. His monthly check wasn't much, but he didn't require much. He considered the stationary bike a good investment.

The training apparatus served its purpose, although he greatly missed the freedom of flying along a country road with the glory of the outdoors enveloping him. He set the bike up in the living room in front of an old 1976 Magnavox console he and his wife had purchased to celebrate their tenth anniversary. The walnut housing gave the old TV the dignity of a quality piece of furniture that the modern flat screens lacked. He had purchased a digital converter at Walmart recently to pick up a few local channels. He scheduled his workout for half past six in the evening so that he could watch the national news, Wheel of Fortune, and Jeopardy. Crime shows, dramas, and comedies did not interest him. He liked old movies, ones that he had seen many times, and he liked the familiarity, routine and educational benefits of the news and game shows.

Like most veteran runners, he discovered he had to brace himself for the challenge of running outdoors through the winter months. He had become an expert of proper layering of clothing to befit the weather conditions. Every morning he would watch the Weather Channel to plan for that day's run. He hated wearing sweat pants and found that medium-length running shorts suited him well even when the temperature was in the forties. After a couple of miles his body warmed up to the extent where he didn't notice the cold against his bare legs. To keep his torso warm he would don a long sleeve t-shirt with a short sleeve t-shirt underneath. His dresser drawers were stuffed full of shirts from all the races he had run. He never pitched them out, even though some had become ragged, stained, and holey.

When the temperature dropped under forty, he reluctantly wore sweat pants, the old gray cotton ones like he had worn in high school in the sixties when he ran for the Martins Ferry Purple Riders. He didn't go in for tights. He considered them too feminine, something a dancer would wear. The most difficult days came when the temperature dropped below twenty degrees and the wind howled. To combat frostbite he would wear long johns under his sweatpants and a heavy, hooded sweatshirt, medium-weight gloves, thick socks, and if need be a ski mask. Even with all of these layers the wind could be a killer.

One cold morning in mid-December he ran six miles along County Road 4 just past Floral Valley. He did not realize a strong wind was at his back. When he turned to head home the breeze hit him smack in the face. He had neglected to wear a ski mask that day. For six miles he plowed through the wind. His face went numb, so he tried to run while clasping the hood against his cheeks. That seemed to help, but then his quads froze from the wind blowing against his sweaty thighs. With four miles to go he could no longer feel the area between his legs. That was one place he did not want damaged by frostbite. He pulled off one of his gloves and stuck it down in his underwear. Everything was numb down there, and now his hand was exposed to the frigid air. He pulled his sleeve over his hand and clasped it. The last two miles along Route 7 the wind blew even harder, so he forced himself to run hard to escape the elements as soon as possible. Unfortunately, the pace caused him to breathe the cold air deeper into his lungs. By the time he got home he felt like a Cro-Magnon man who had just been chiseled out of a hunk of ice. He couldn't stop coughing. After he thawed out, he checked to see if all of his parts were still attached. Thank God, they were.

𐊗𐊗𐊗𐊗𐊗

One week before Christmas on a dreary Tuesday evening, he decided to drive out to Alisha's restaurant and try his luck again with Rita Marling. The sky brooded with heavy gray cumulus clouds, and he feared getting caught in a snowstorm. When he entered the dining area she spotted him, and her smile flashed like a lighthouse across a stormy sea. He sat down at a table for two in the corner.

She marched over and planted her hands on her hips. "Where have you been, Angelo? I haven't seen you for almost a month. Did you forget about me?"

"No. Of course not," he sputtered. "In November I put away my bike for the winter."

"You don't have a driver's licence?"

"Yes. Of course I do."

"It took you a month to decide to drive out and see me? That makes me feel real special. What took you so long?"

He felt his face flush. "I've been busy."

"Getting ready for your marathon, no doubt."

He could not tell by the tone of her voice if she was angry or just joking with him. He said, "Yes, I've been in training, but I've been thinking about you."

She sat down in the chair across from him and leaned her chin against her clasped fingers. "What kind of thoughts have you had about me?"

"Good thoughts."

"Good in what way?"

"What do you mean?"

"Wholesome good or naughty good?"

The old man gulped and glanced around. Several customers were looking their way. A restaurant wasn't the right place for this kind of talk. "I was wondering if you would like to get together."

She batted her eyes. "Are you asking me out on a date?"

"Sure."

"Dinner and dancing?"

The old man opened his mouth to speak but hesitated. He was a terrible dancer. He did not want to make a fool of himself on their first date. "Could we start with just dinner?"

Rita yawned. "Just dinner? Where would you take me?"

The old man said the first restaurant that popped into his mind: "Bob Evans." Immediately he knew he had made a blunder. He liked Bob Evans and lived about a half mile from the one on Route 7 but now realized it wasn't a very romantic choice.

"Bob Evans," Rita blurted and then giggled.

The old man closed eyes and shook his head. His determination and perseverance could not compensate for his lack of refinement. Oh well, he thought, I am what I am.

"I'll think about it," Rita said.

The old man lifted his hands slightly from the table. "Don't think too hard. I know I'm not a prize. Just an old, retired mill worker."

Rita shook her head, moved her hand toward his mouth, and touched his lips with her index finger. "Don't say that. You're more than just an old, retired mill worker."

He lifted her finger from his lips and said, "I am?"

"You're a man with a dream—you want to run a marathon, and you're willing to work hard to accomplish that dream. I respect that. When are you going to take me to Bob Evans?"

The old man's mind whirled as he tried to process her words. He didn't expect that answer or her sudden assent to his invitation to dinner. "What night are you off next week?"

"Tuesday."

"Tuesday is good for me."

After finishing his dinner that evening, the old man drove home in a snow storm. His Dodge Duster spun and skidded all over the road, but he kept a slow, steady speed up the hills and crept around the turns. Despite the stress of driving through hazardous conditions, he felt like a teenage boy who just got a date with the best looking girl in the school. But more than that he possessed a tremendous sense of affirmation—the kind of feeling one gets when another believes in him.

On that Sunday's long run the old man wanted to attempt eighteen miles. He picked up the boy at his house and they ran across the two bridges and onto the asphalt path along the river to the deer crossing sign. The whole way the old man's left heel hurt, and his Achilles tendon on that same leg nagged him with a slight shooting pain with every step. He worried that the tendon may tear at any second.

At first he blamed it on the cold weather. Ever since November ushered in cooler temperatures his heel bothered him during the first mile but went away once things got warmed up. In the mornings when he stepped out of bed the heel hurt for the first half hour or so. Now he feared it was more than just a sore heel from a stone bruise. In all likelihood plantar faciitis had set in. The Achilles tendon pain was an even greater concern. If he strained or tore that tendon, he was in big trouble. He also realized everything was connected: The fascia on the bottom of his foot tied into his heel which was connected to the Achilles tendon. One thing affected the other. There were always balances and counter-balances in running. The body worked as a unit. If one part became damaged, then the body had to compensate. The old man guessed that the heel problem had triggered the Achilles pain.

"I usually don't complain," the old man said, "but I think my heel pain is much worse than I first believed."

"That's not good," the boy said. "How bad is it?"

"Usually by this point in the run it fades away, but not today. Now the pain is shooting up through my Achilles."

"Do you need to walk."

"No," the old man said. "But I probably will stop at your house. Eighteen miles is out of the question today."

"Did you ever have this kind of injury before?"

"Yes. Many years ago. It took months to heal. I probably should go see a physical therapist or a podiatrist."

"You should go see the Witch Doctor."

"Who?"

"The Witch Doctor. That's what they call him, anyway. He works magic with running injuries."

The old man had never heard of this person. Most family physicians offered the same solution to almost every running injury: take six weeks off until the pain goes away and then start running again at a shorter distance. This prescription was unacceptable to a person preparing for a marathon. If a runner took time off for every ache or pain encountered, he would never train. Serious distance runners faced the fact that battling minor injuries was a daily factor in their training routine. Successful distance runners learned to manage these constant aches and pains effectively. Certain specialists and therapists became locally well known for their skill in treating running injuries without interruption to the training program. Perhaps this mysterious healer was one of them.

"How did you hear about this Witch Doctor?"

"Our top runner, Justin Lewis, went to see him with Achilles tendon problems. Justin said the Witch Doctor's methods were very painful but effective. He never missed a day of practice. At the end of the season he qualified for the state meet."

"Really." Perhaps, the old man thought, this Witch Doctor knows some secrets. "Where is his office?"

"In St. Clairsville. He works out of his garage."

"Out of his garage? He must not be a real doctor."

"I'm not sure, but it is very difficult to get an appointment with him."

"Hmmmm." The old man wondered about this miracle worker. It is possible this man was gifted with special knowledge and techniques. Legends like this usually contained threads of truth based on solid results. Besides, the old man thought, I would rather take a chance with an unlicensed legend than be told to take six weeks off by a physician with ten diplomas hanging on his wall. "It's difficult getting in to see the Witch Doctor, eh?"

"Yes," the boy said. "Very difficult. You must know someone."

"I know you."

"But I'm not very important."

"You are very important to me."

The boy smiled. "Let me talk to Justin's father. He knows the Witch Doctor."

"Put in a good word for me," the old man said. "I will definitely need a miracle worker to get through this marathon training."

On Tuesday evening the old man drove out into the country to pick up Rita Marling for their dinner date. By six p.m. night had already arrived, and a brisk wind made the mid-thirty temperatures seem more like the teens. She lived near the Holly Memorial Cemetery along Route 250 in a modest ranch home, white siding with black shutters. On the way out he had worried about spending the next two to three hours with her. What would they talk about? Would there be uncomfortable silences? At Alisha's Restaurant customers drew her attention away from him. Now they would be focused on each other. It had been a long time since he exercised his conversational skills with a woman in this kind of setting. He had never been a Casanova. He and his late wife fell in love as kids in high school and married while they were still in their teens. He wondered if Rita Marling would think he was a rube. He felt like kicking himself for these kinds of thoughts. Why worry about it? If the date is a flop, so what? I should be more worried if we fall for each other, he told himself. Then he would have to give up the solitary life to which he had become accustomed. Making more room in his daily routine for a sweetheart could complicate things. That must be a tendency with old, single men, he thought. We become very guarded in parceling out time and giving up ground acquired in bachelorhood.

To his great surprise, Rita Marling was ready and raring to go when he greeted her at the door. His late wife was late for everything, which conditioned him to be patient and longsuffering. He gave up trying to change his wife early in their marriage. He discovered some things you cannot change about a person. Of

40

course, he knew that he was not the ideal man, and his wife often reminded him of that fact. However, she never tried to change him. Maybe that is why they had loved each other for so many years.

During the twenty minute drive back to town Rita talked about her day waiting on tables. The old man focused on driving and listening. He was glad she was in a talkative mood. That meant less mental effort for him, although her chattering made him wonder if she was even interested in his life. By the time they reached Bob Evans at the south end of town, she had run out of things to say and finally asked him what he had been up to all day.

The old man thought about his day and how boring the account of it would be to someone like Rita Marling. He had spent an hour fixing his vacuum cleaner. Then he read running magazines for another hour. He changed the oil in his car and cleaned and vacuumed the vehicle in preparation for their date. Then he watched an old John Wayne movie. No doubt she would fall asleep if he went through the trivialities of his day. Instead, he decided to tell her about his injury and all the grief it caused him. She seemed very concerned.

The hostess sat them at a table at the back of the restaurant near a window. Rita slid out of her dark gray coat with black fur around the collar and cuffs. She wore a silky black shirt that draped nicely over her slim but shapely figure. She slung the coat over the back of the chair and sat down.

Rita asked, "Could the injury prevent you from running the marathon?"

He nodded. "Tendonitis can be tricky. It will continue to worsen if I don't cut back on my training. Even if I do the right things, it may take six to eight weeks to heal. I'm worried most about my Achilles tendon. I don't have the flexibility I used to have. If it would snap, my running days may be over."

"Why take the chance? Why don't you just quit running? "

"Quit running?" The question astounded him, but then he realized a non-runner wouldn't understand how preposterous the query was. "No. I couldn't just give it up."

"Listen, I know an old man who's a greeter at Wal-Mart. He was an obsessed runner like you. Now he limps badly because his knees and hips are in such bad shape. Why not take up another sport? Try bowling or golf or tennis."

The old man shook his head. "I might end up like your friend at Wal-Mart, but until my body betrays me, I'll keep plugging away at it."

Rita Marling shrugged. "It just doesn't make sense to me. You are a very peculiar man, Angelo."

"You think I'm strange?"

"Not strange. Uncommon. I find you interesting. That's why I wanted to go out with you."

"Really?" The old man never considered himself to be interesting or uncommon. "If that's true, why did you turn me down the first time I asked you out?"

Rita smiled, her white teeth flashing. "I had a date with another man that night. You and I aren't going steady, right?"

"No. We hardly know each other. Besides, I have another girlfriend too."

Rita's mouth fell open. "Is that right? Who is she?"

"She's a very demanding lady and jealous too."

"Hmmmph. How serious is this relationship?"

"Very serious."

Rita crossed her arms. "I'm surprised she allowed you to go out with me. Tell me her name. I might know her"

"Lady Marathon." The old man smiled.

Rita's dark brown eyes widened. "I take back what I said about you a minute ago."

"What? That I'm uncommon?"

"No. That you're not strange."

They both laughed.

To the old man's surprise, the next several hours went very quickly. After dinner they drove back to her house and watched a movie on DVD about Abraham Lincoln. Although it was a newer movie, the old man enjoyed it. He liked history. Before he said good night, he even kissed her on the lips. It wasn't a passionate kiss, more like a friendly kiss, but one that felt quite enjoyable despite its brevity. Driving home, he wondered if he and Rita Marling were falling for each other.

𝄞𝄞𝄞𝄞𝄞

The Witch Doctor lived along Barton Road about a mile before entering the town of St. Clairsville. The old man's appointment had been scheduled for four o'clock in the afternoon on the tenth of January, a bitterly cold day. The bare trees that lined the road along the ridge swayed against the leaden sky. When the old man pulled into the driveway, he wasn't sure if he had found the right house but then noticed the unattached garage that served as the Witch Doctor's office. It was a redbrick structure with green garage doors, just as Manny had described it. A door on the side of the garage opened, and two figures emerged—a teenager and a guy probably in his forties. The old man figured they were a father and son seeing the healer about some injury the son had incurred in his particular sport. As the old man stepped out of the car, the pain in his heel jolted up through his Achilles tendon. He closed his eyes, took a deep breath, and limped toward the entrance.

As he passed the man and boy, he nodded and said, "Excuse me."

They stopped and eyed him.

The old man pointed at the door. "Does this guy know what he's doing?"

The man smiled. He had thinning brown hair, gray sideburns and wore brown-rimmed glasses. "There's nobody like him. Maybe not the friendliest guy you'll ever meet, but so what. My son never missed a step of training because of him."

"Is he a real doctor?"

The man shrugged. "Nobody knows and nobody asks." They turned and walked toward their car.

The old man faced the door and wondered if he should knock. If it's an office, he should walk right in, he thought. He turned the

43

knob and entered. The room was bright, lit by fluorescent lights which hung from chains attached to ceiling rafters. There was a thread-bare brown couch immediately to his right facing an old-style portable television on a black plastic stand with a stack of magazines next to it. An assortment of exercise equipment was spaced around the room, and a stationary bike sat off to the left. A weight machine and free weights took up most of the space in the back. On the floor he noticed different sized balls and Styrofoam cylinders. In the back right corner he spotted a black man staring into an open refrigerator. The man turned and faced him holding a bottle of water, and the refrigerator door closed behind him. He was short and squat with a shaved head and a thin black mustache. He wore a dark blue warm-up suit with a Nike swoosh on the left breast. The old man had a hard time guessing his age.

"I'm Angelo," the old man said. "I've got an appointment."

The black man grunted a greeting, but the old man didn't quite understand. Then he motioned with his finger to come nearer. "Walk to me." His voice was gravely.

The old man took about four steps, but then the Witch Doctor raised his hand like a cop stopping traffic. "Walk on your heels the rest of the way."

"My heels?" The old man couldn't believe it. The pain was searing enough trying to walk normally. Not wanting to appear wimpy, he gritted his teeth and raised the balls of his feet in the air. It took all of his self-control not to scream. It felt like someone had rammed a hot poker up through his left heel, but he walked haltingly toward the Witch Doctor.

"That's far enough," the black man said.

The old man tottered to a stop, blinking back the water that pooled in his eyes.

"My guess is you've got plantar fasciitis and Achilles tendonitis."

"Good guess."

"From what I can see, it's a fairly severe case. Do this." He stuck his hands out like a sleep walker and squatted. "Try to keep your heels on the floor."

The position didn't look that difficult. The old man stuck out his hands and lowered himself.

"No. That's not right," the Witch Doctor growled. "Keep your heels flat on the floor."

The old man realized his heels had risen up when he had squatted, but no matter how hard he tried, he could not lower his heels to the floor without losing his balance. "I can't do it."

"Of course you can't. Your muscles are imbalanced. Whenever there's an imbalance in your body, injuries are bound to occur. The main cause of imbalances is overuse of certain muscles. You're a distance runner, correct?"

The old man nodded. "You can tell a lot by a few observations."

The black man met his gaze. "I've seen this sort of thing a thousand times."

"Can you help me?"

He pointed to a massage table to the right. "Take off your shoes, socks, and your pants and have a seat."

The old man quickly untied his shoes and peeled off his socks. He had put on sweatpants with running shorts underneath. He slid out of the gray sweatpants and hopped up onto the table.

The therapist walked to him and lifted both feet until his legs straightened. He shook the right leg and then pushed the heel of his hand against the old man's toes, pressing his foot back. "Push against my hand."

The old man obeyed, but he was beginning to fear the Witch Doctor was sadistic. He hoped his first impression was mistaken.

"Harder."

"Okay." The old man pushed the Witch Doctor's hand as hard as he could with the ball of his foot.

"Now the other one." He repeated the same procedure with the old man's left leg and foot. Then he dropped the left leg and lifted the right leg again. "What happened to this leg?"

"It's fine. The pain is in my left leg."

The Witch Doctor's brow knotted. "I know that. Answer my question. What happened to the right leg?"

Could he be talking about my sciatica, the old man wondered. "Well, years ago I had severe sciatica problems in that leg."

"Yes. That's what I figured. The right leg is weaker than the left leg because of the past injury. The left leg compensates for its partner. That's why you have tendonitis in your heel and Achilles."

"I want to run a marathon in May. Do you think it's possible to train through an injury like this?"

"Depends. How much pain can you take?" The black man reached down, lifted his left foot, and squeezed his heel.

The old man sucked in a quick breath of air as the jolt shot up through his Achilles. He gritted his teeth and said, "I can take a lot of pain."

The Witch Doctor smiled, his eyes shining. "We'll see." He grasped his left calf and slid his hand down the Achilles tendon, around the heel, and brushed his thumb across the arch. "You've put in a lot of miles over the years, haven't you?"

"I've been running since I was a boy."

"You've accumulated an extraordinary amount of scar tissue. Imbalance and scar tissue—those are your problems."

"Can they be solved?"

"I know a few tricks to help you."

"But can I continue to train while you treat me?"

"I insist that you do."

The old man wondered if he heard him right. Maybe this guy isn't so bad after all, he thought.

The Witch Doctor stepped back and motioned the old man to slide off of the massage table. "We'll start with trigger points first. Watch what I do." He sat on the floor and placed his left calf on a foam roller and crossed his right leg over. With his hands behind him on the floor, he lifted up his rear end and swayed back and forth so the roller massaged his left calf muscle. "As you do this, you will notice tender spots on the muscle. You need to focus on these spots until the pain subsides. These are called trigger points. Here, you try it." The therapist jumped to his feet and waved his hand at the Styrofoam roller.

The old man repeated the same procedure with the Styrofoam roller. He was amazed at how the pressure affected the trigger points on his leg. He found many spots that needed massaging, but after a minute or two the pain subsided and his leg became more relaxed. The Witch Doctor instructed him to work on all the trigger points up to his buttocks on both legs. By the time he finished, his legs felt rejuvenated, although the heel and Achilles pain were still quite noticeable.

The Witch Doctor gave him the end of a rubber medical hose and then stepped about eight feet back, holding the other end high above his head and keeping the hose taut between them. "Squat down slowly and keep your heels flat on the ground. Don't worry about keeping your balance. Trust me. I'll keep you from falling over."

The old man took a deep breath and blew it out. He lowered himself slowly with the stretched hose between them preventing him from falling backwards. He hoped this wasn't a trick. If the Witch Doctor let go, he would fly backwards and smash his skull against the floor. By leaning with the support of the hose he could keep his heels flat on the ground.

"Do about ten squats," the black man said. "Make sure you keep your heels on the ground."

Up and down the old man went, holding tightly to the hose. By the time he finished, his trust in the therapist had increased.

"I'll send a hose home with you. I want you to do this every day. Tie the end of the hose to something about seven feet high. Work your way up to thirty repetitions. With time your muscles will become more balanced."

The therapist showed him a number of other exercises to help balance his muscles, ones he had seen before in running magazines. Then he ordered the old man to get on the stationary bike and pedal at a good pace for ten minutes. He told him he wanted his muscles good and warm before he began the treatment that would help remove scar tissue. As the old man pedaled the bike, fears about the Witch Doctor began to subside. Maybe he wasn't sadistic. He just had an unusual manner about him. Perhaps these legends about this healer were true.

Next the therapist pointed to a darkened doorway at the back of the garage. "That's the ASTYM Therapy Room. Follow me."

As the old man gazed into the blackness of the doorway, an eerie prickling crawled up his spine. "What's ASTYM therapy?"

"You'll find out." The black man strode to the doorway, reached into the darkness, and flipped on the light. It was a small, windowless room, with a massage table in the middle and white shelves on the back wall. "Climb up on the table and lie on your belly. Let your feet hang over the edge."

As the old man obeyed, the Witch Doctor walked to the white shelves, reached, and pulled down a plastic jar with a big round black cap. He walked back to the massage table and dipped his fingers into the jar. The old man could see that the contents were some kind of liniment. He took a relaxing breath. Good, the old man thought. ASTYM must be some kind of massage therapy. I could use a good massage.

The therapist took the oily liniment and coated the old man's left foot, ankle, calf and hamstring. For a few minutes he rubbed the substance into his skin, massaging the muscles and tendons. Then he walked back to the shelves, tore off a paper towel from a roll and wiped his hands. That was quick, the old man thought. Massages usually last longer than a few minutes. The black man reached onto the highest shelf and pulled down something that looked like a shoe horn. It was about six or eight inches long and made of clear plastic with rounded edges.

"What's that for?" the old man asked.

"This is what I use to break up the scar tissue. Face forward. It's better for you not to watch."

The old man's heart sunk in his chest. He focused straight ahead and gripped the edge of the massage table. What was he going to do with that plastic tool? He felt the Witch Doctor grasp the top of his foot. Then the hard plastic edge of the tool dug into his heel and scraped toward his arch. He almost screamed. It felt like someone had taken a radial saw to his foot. Please, please God make him stop, the old man prayed. But the Witch Doctor did not stop. He kept scraping from the top of his heel down through his arch again and again, moving the instrument slightly each time to cover a new area. The old man's fingers turned white from gripping the end of the massage table.

"Do you hear that crackling noise?" the Witch Doctor asked.

The old man swallowed, trying to regain his voice. "Y Y Y eesss. I can hear it. Are you pulverizing my bones?"

The black man laughed heartily. "No. Your bones are fine. That's scar tissue breaking up."

After completing the work on the arch, the Witch Doctor continued the same severe scraping up through his Achilles tendon and calf. The pain did not decrease. The old man's eyes watered and tears dripped over the lower lids. He had to concentrate on breathing long slow breaths to keep from crying like a baby. Finally the scraping was finished.

"Get off the table and walk into the other room," the black man commanded.

When the old man stepped onto the indoor-outdoor carpeting, he was shocked that the heel pain had suddenly decreased. He walked into the bigger room barely limping.

"How's it feel."

"Much better."

"I want you to go home and run five miles on it."

"Seriously?"

"Seriously. I've broken up some of the scar tissue. It needs to be carried off through the blood system. Drink plenty of water to help wash out the toxins. You'll notice when you get home you will be black and blue."

The old man glanced at his calf, Achilles tendon, and heel. They were bright red like a severe sunburn. "Yes. No doubt they will be bruised."

"Don't worry about it. It will go away in two days. I'll see you again in three days."

49

"For more scraping?"

"Of course. It takes about six sessions to eliminate the scar tissue. Do all the exercises I showed you and run five to seven miles a day. If all things go well, we'll increase your mileage next week."

The old man nodded, happy the therapy was over. He stepped into his sweat pants, pulled them up. After putting his socks and shoes back on, he extracted his wallet from a front pocket. "How much do I owe you?"

"Seventy-five dollars a session. Cash only please."

That's a high price to pay for my suffering, the old man thought, but he gladly paid, reasoning that miracles didn't come cheaply nowadays. And rarely are good things accomplished without suffering.

𐀪𐀪𐀪𐀪𐀪

The next several weeks went by quickly as the old man kept his appointments with the Witch Doctor. To his dismay the treatments did not become more tolerable. The sessions reminded him of the dentist appointments of his childhood before the widely accepted practice of using Novacane to numb the mouth. To get through them, he tried to put himself in a place of tranquility—running along the beach, walking through new-fallen snow, feeling the cleansing of a spring rain. He told himself that learning to endure pain through mental distraction would ultimately contribute to his success as a marathoner. The last six miles of a marathon require an incredible high tolerance for pain, especially if the runner is pushing it to the limit.

To his amazement, the treatments worked. He could tell the difference on his first run that very afternoon after the first session. By the end of the third week the pain in both the heel and the Achilles tendon was almost gone. The Witch Doctor told him it would take six weeks for the pain to completely disappear. The old man no longer viewed the black healer as sadistic. Quite the opposite—his respect increased for the man tenfold as he recovered

50

and his runs lengthened. The afternoon of his last treatment he ran a ten miler, and the following Sunday he and the boy ran twelve miles along the river trail to Warwood and back. At the beginning of February as the daylight lengthened, so did the old man's hope that spring would bring a productive season of training culminating in a successful marathon at the beginning of May.

His love life also improved as the bleak days of winter ended. Dinner dates with Rita Marling became a regular part of his weekly schedule. However, Rita insisted they venture out of Martins Ferry and patronize other establishments besides Bob Evans—Applebees and the Outback Steakhouse at the Ohio Valley Mall, and the Olive Garden and Cheddar's at the Highlands, to name a few. The old man still refused to go dancing with her and did not protest when she informed him that she could always find a dancing partner if he refused to go. He did not want to rob her of this hobby. She loved to dance, and he loved to run. Of course, she understood that she could not interfere with his training. Running came first. She didn't seem to mind. Perhaps they were of the age when independence took priority over losing oneself in another. For now they enjoyed one another's company and looked forward to getting together. With time maybe would they fall more deeply in love.

On the last Sunday of February he and the boy went out for a final run together. Track started the first week of March, and the boy's parents insisted that he no longer train with the old man on Sundays once practice started. The old man had worked his way back up to fourteen miles, and the boy, despite his parents' restrictions, insisted he run the entire distance with him. To the old man the day seemed like a wonderful gift from God: a clear blue sky, temperatures in the mid-forties, and a good friend running by his side. They both trotted along in mid-length shorts and long-sleeved t-shirts.

"You were right about the Witch Doctor," the old man said. "He is a miracle worker."

"I am glad he worked his magic on you. Was it painful?"

"Pray that you never have to go through ASTYM therapy."

"That bad, eh?"

"Yes, but worth every bit of the agony I suffered."

"Now you will be able to run the Pittsburgh Marathon and qualify for Boston."

"I don't count my chickens too soon, Manny."

"I will count them for you. I believe in you."

"I'm glad you have faith in me, but I must remain humble."

"I understand."

"The marathon is much bigger than me. If I complete the challenge successfully, it is not because I was a great man and overcame the distance. Rather, it is because I was a humble man and was given the gift."

"What gift?"

"The gift of running these long distances. It is an especially gracious gift to receive at my age."

"Do you think I have been given this gift?"

"Yes. You have the talent to be a great runner."

"I also have a goal."

"Is it a great goal?"

"I don't know," the boy said.

"Always choose a goal that is bigger than you. What is your goal?"

"I want to break the school record in the 3200 meter run."

"That is a great goal. That record is more than forty years old. A friend of mine set it back in the seventies. Do you know the time you would have to run to beat it?"

"Yes. 9:11. Do you think that goal will keep me humble?"

"No doubt. To break 9:11 you will have to be one of the best high school two milers in the country."

Stopping in front of the boy's house, they finished the run. The old man wished him luck in the upcoming track season. Then they shook hands and said goodbye. As the old man jogged home, he felt sad. He had looked forward to every Sunday afternoon's run with the boy. Now he faced the two most difficult months of training alone.

🏃🏃🏃🏃🏃

The following Sunday the old man attempted a sixteen miler. It was a dreary, overcast day in early March. The winds rushed across the river and blew sleet into his face as he ran along the trail toward the town of Warwood. Because the temperature hovered in the mid-thirties, he had put on sweat pants and a well-worn, hooded sweatshirt. The cold drizzle slowly but surely soaked into his garments creating a growing heaviness. At the four-mile mark he spied large black birds with four-or-five-feet wingspans circling above him. Noting their ugly red heads, he identified them as turkey vultures. They roosted on top of an old five-story, brick building along the asphalt trail by the river. He wondered if they were eyeing him. Those birds sensed when an animal was about to die. Their presence made him shudder.

A couple of miles later he noticed a bearded man running in his direction. He didn't expect to greet another runner along the path on this kind of dismal day. As he neared the fellow, he waved and said hi, but the runner ignored him. Then he noticed the guy had on headphones. The old man hated headphones. To him they defeated one of the purposes of running—experiencing the sounds and sights of the outdoors. Headphones kept you in your own little customized media library. You might as well stay indoors and run on a treadmill or go to your local fitness center and put time in on an elliptical trainer. Running meant freedom, and headphones were a chain linked to the electronic-virtual world. Besides, the old man was convinced headphones were dangerous. They blocked out all sound. He wanted to be able to hear cars coming behind him or friends calling his name. No doubt people considered him out of sync with the times, but by Jove, he would never be caught with headphones on.

By the time the old man reached the turn-around point at the Pike Island Dam, the sleet had soaked him, the wind had chilled him, and the loneliness had depressed him. He felt like he was out in the middle of the river treading waters that were dark and deep. He turned and headed in the direction from which he came. Eight miles to go, he thought. I wish the boy was running with me. Will I make it back? He tried to make an accurate assessment of his circumstances: He was a long way from home, wet, cold, and tired. He glanced around and noticed the freezing drizzle had stopped. Across the river to the west the sky had turned a lighter gray. Then he focused on his heel and Achilles tendon. He was definitely tired but felt no soreness at all where the tendonitis had once threatened to end his marathon training. He had to admit that his right leg felt good too—no nagging sciatica pain for many months.

He heard the blare of a horn and glanced up to see a familiar car go by and the flash of a hand. It was George "the Hammer" Mason, an old running buddy and fellow mill worker. In his younger years George and he competed in many road races together. Unfortunately, all the miles hammered the Hammer, causing many severe joint problems. With each step, the old man realized how lucky he was to still be running. The attrition of this sport for runners over sixty was extremely high. Many encountered joint problems, others heart problems, and still others back problems. A bird flew over the old man's head and landed on the branch of a small tree along the trail. He noticed its orange breast—a robin! It was the first robin the old man had seen this year. The sun broke through the clouds in the western sky, and his surroundings lit up, colors pouring forth covering the drab gray. He smiled and thought, is a man ever really alone? With all the birds and animals and people surrounding him, weren't they all part of something greater? The old man pondered these things for the next several miles, and before he knew it, he had arrived home.

𝆺𝆺𝆺𝆺𝆺

The days of March slipped slowly by. On the second Sunday of the month he ran a seventeen miler; on the third, an eighteen miler; on the fourth, a nineteen miler. His joints always hurt the day after the long run. Popping a couple of aspirin usually made the pain subside. Certainly, joint pain was normal for a sixty-three-year old putting in that kind of mileage. He didn't worry about it. On the last day of March he turned sixty-four. He felt like he was in great shape. Although he hadn't done much speed work, he wondered what kind of time he could run for a 5K. No one had beaten him locally in his age group for years at that distance. His best 5k time since turning sixty was 19:52. Could he break 19:50? He had read articles in the running magazines attesting that marathon training increased a runner's VO2 Max. Now he was curious.

The local running club organized a race on the first Saturday in April, the day before Easter—the Webark No-Kill Animal Shelter 5K in Glen Dale, West Virginia. The old man loved the course. It started at Reynolds Memorial Hospital but quickly veered off on a country road that went slightly uphill to the turn-around point and then slightly downhill back to the finish. It was a fast course. Perhaps he needed a break from these long Sunday runs, and a speed workout would do him good. Besides, it was a great cause— saving abandoned animals from euthanasia. With the marathon a little over a month away, he needed one more long run, a twenty miler, to complete his training plan. Then he would begin to taper. If he did the twenty miler on the second Sunday in April, would the timing be right? That would give him three weeks before the marathon. That seemed reasonable. On Saturday he would head down to Glen Dale to see how fast he could run a 5K road race.

The week plodded by as he alternated ten-mile runs with ninety-minute stationary bike sessions. Early Saturday morning he drove into the country to pick up Rita. On their Thursday evening dinner date she had expressed interest in accompanying him to the race. This delighted the old man at first, but as Saturday neared, he wondered if it was such a good idea. All of his running buddies would have something to say. Most thought he was a dyed-in-the-wool bachelor with little interest in the opposite sex. They would raise their eyebrows, wink, and taunt him. On race day he didn't need distractions. Of course, Rita's good looks would make some of them jealous. That would be just fine with him.

Her presence also increased the pressure to run well. Why did that bother him? He'd run hundreds of races and excelled ninety-five percent of the time. Only once in a great while did he ever crumble, and then only because of severe heat, or a tactical error, or a bad cold. Deep down, though, he knew that success in past races meant nothing. The starting line was a place where you had to prove yourself all over again. No one counted on past efforts. Every race was a test. If you weren't willing to push yourself to the limit, then you would be humbled by those of less ability who were willing to give their all. The old man didn't mind getting beat by anyone if he gave his best effort. He despised the times when he yielded to mental weakness which resulted in a lackluster finish. The gleam in the eye of an opponent he should have beaten created a discontent within that could not be rectified until he toed the starting line of the next race. The starting line offered both the hope of redemption and the fear of failure.

As he weaved in and out of the crowd to get nearer to the front of the starting line, nervous excitement fluttered his stomach. It was a feeling that set him on edge, but also one he craved. No matter how insignificant the race, he always experienced this wonderful nervous anticipation. It was addictive. Some runners showed up at every starting line of every race in the Ohio Valley because they loved the charge they got out of it. He usually lined up in the second or third row behind a few young guns. He did not have the speed any more to start in the first row although he would probably finish in the top fifteen. Inexperienced runners sprinted the first hundred yards or so and then petered out. Then there were the young kids who just got in the way. Why their parents allowed them or even encouraged them to line up in the front row he could never understand. They were lucky if they didn't get trampled. Unbelievably, there were walkers who also tried to get a spot in front. You did not want to line up behind several front-row walkers. You end up being corralled for the first hundred yards by a slow-moving, human fence. Experience had taught the old man to pick out the young studs and fall in behind them. They shot out like cheetahs and he followed in their wake.

The gun sent the runners off to a fairly smooth start. Several hundred yards later when the lead pack turned onto the country road, the old man figured he was in about thirtieth place. That was fine. By the first mile he moved up into the top twenty. The old man chuckled to himself. Most runners did not understand pacing and the importance of even splits. Going out too fast was the most common tactical error. Runners who formed this bad habit used half their energy in that first mile. That left fifty percent for the final two miles. The old man knew an even pace made for a much more efficient use of the body's fuel. Psychologically, right pacing helped the runner keep mentally tough for the most difficult final portion of the race. Relax and enjoy the first two miles as much as possible, the old man told himself. Then be prepared to push through the agony of the last mile.

At the turn around, about halfway through the race, the old man spotted a familiar figure—a man of medium height with dark brown hair and a mustache. He wore a white tank top and purple shorts. The old man tried to place him in his memory: Of course—Manny's high school coach. After the old man circled the cone, it didn't take long to catch him.

He decided not to fly by him without a word. That would be arrogant. He pulled up beside him and said, "Good morning, Coach Silvers."

The coach glanced at the old man. "Oh . . . hi," he managed to say between breaths. "Angelo, right?"

"That's right. It's been a few months since we ran together. No track meet today?"

"No . . . we have . . . practice at noon. First invitational . . . next Saturday."

"Good luck."

"Thanks."

The old man could tell by Silvers' breathing that he was starting to falter. He picked up his pace and left the coach in his dust. The know-it-all marathoner went out too fast, the old man concluded. Now he's paying the price. Peering down the road a few hundred yards, he spotted a man dressed in a green warm up suit peering down at something in his hand. He guessed the guy must be the split caller for the two-mile mark. He checked his breathing. It was becoming more stressed but not harsh. *Stay relaxed. Maintain your form. Keep the legs turning over quickly.* He kept repeating these words like a mantra to himself. *Stay relaxed. Maintain your form. Keep the legs turning over quickly.* He passed the two-mile mark and the man in green called out his time: 12:45. Wow, great time, he thought.

Knowing that he was on track to break 19:50 motivated him to push the last mile. He caught three more people before rounding the final turn. With about one hundred yards to go, he squinted to see the large digital clock to the right of the chute—19:30-31-32-33-34 . . . He pumped his arms harder and tried to lift his knees. The pain wracked his body. There in the midst of the crowd that lined the road Rita stood cheering and shouting. Despite the agony, he pushed himself to the end and crossed in 19:48. He slowed to a stop and leaned on his knees to catch his breath. The time was amazing—a new personal record for his age group. He walked haltingly, feeling exhausted but exhilarated.

At the end of the chute, he turned to look for Rita. She filtered through the crowd and ran toward him with open arms. This surprised the old man, but as she neared he spread his arms and hugged her.

"You really ran well," Rita said. "I counted you in thirteenth place."

"Thirteenth? Are you sure?" The old man wasn't superstitious, but he never did like the number thirteen.

"Pretty sure." Rita stepped back and smiled, that big smile that had first captured his heart many months ago. "Aren't you happy with your place?"

"Very happy. Finishing in the top fifteen in a race this big is quite good for anyone my age."

The old man glanced to his right and noticed Coach Silvers crossing the finish line. "Good job, Coach," he said as the man plodded through the chute.

Silvers glanced up and said, "Thanks."

"Who is that?" Rita asked.

"My friend Emmanuel's high school coach. I caught up with him about halfway through the race, but he couldn't keep my pace."

Rita stared at the man as he made his way to the end of the chute. "He looks familiar."

At the awards ceremony in the back parking lot of the hospital, the sun beamed down from a clear blue sky and the temperature warmed up nicely into the sixties. Several of the old man's buddies greeted him and then eyed Rita Marling. The old man introduced her as his girlfriend. He could tell they were impressed, and Rita enjoyed the attention, batting her eyes and smiling that gorgeous smile at the admirers. What a great day he was having with a wonderful lady by his side.

Coach Silvers walked up to the old man and extended his hand. "Nice job, Angelo. You had a great race."

"Thanks. I was happy with my effort. You did well too."

Silvers shook his head. "No. No. I trained through this one. I'm getting ready for the Pittsburgh Marathon in May. This was just a workout to me. I can run a full minute faster."

The old man didn't have much respect for runners who made excuses. His philosophy was to accept your effort, good or bad, and embrace it. Take full responsibility for it. If it was a poor effort, let it burn inside and use it for motivation for the next race.

"Excuse me," Rita said. "Am I invisible?"

"Forgive me," the old man said. "Rita Marling, this is Coach Silvers, Martins Ferry High School's cross country coach."

Silvers extended his hand. "Very nice to meet such a pretty lady."

Rita took his hand. "You look so familiar. Are you from around here?"

"I'm originally from St. Clairsville. I know you from somewhere. What high school did you attend?"

"Martins Ferry."

"When did you graduate?"

"1978."

"There you go," the Coach said. "We graduated the same year. Did you ever go to the Wheeling Park dances?"

"All the time." Rita raised her finger. "Now I remember. I think I danced with you once."

The coach smiled, a light of recognition brightening his eyes. "Yes. We did dance together. That was a long time ago. Funny how those high school memories stick with us."

Just then the race director called Silvers' name to come forward to get his award—first place for the age group fifty through fifty-four.

"Nice meeting you. And again, Angelo, great race. Next time I'll have to rest to give myself a chance against you." Silvers turned and walked toward the awards table.

"I'll be at the Pittsburgh Marathon too. Surely, you will rest for that one," the old man called out, but Silvers, already several steps away, apparently did not hear him.

On the way home Rita reached over, patted the old man's thigh and asked, "Do you think you can beat Coach Silvers in the marathon?"

"I believe I can, but believing and doing are two different things. The proof is in the doing."

"But he's ten years younger than you. Doesn't that give him a great advantage?"

"It does. He's got about a ten percent advantage."

"Why ten percent?"

"After the age of thirty-five a man loses about one percent of his strength per year. I've lost about thirty percent of the strength of my

60

youth. He's lost about twenty percent. That gives him a ten percent advantage."

Rita lifted her hand from his thigh and rubbed the old man's bicep. "Despite the years, you are still a very strong man. Is that why you believe you can beat him?"

The old man enjoyed her touch. "Age is not the only factor. You must add talent, determination, and hard work into the equation."

"You are one of the hardest workers I know."

"And you are one of the best looking women I know."

She patted his shoulder. "Believe me, I work hard at that."

"Did you really dance with Coach Silvers in high school?"

Rita raised her eyebrows. "Yes. And from what I remember, he was a very good dancer."

The old man wasn't pleased with her answer. He grew silent and his mind drifted to the Outer Banks. He remembered running along the beach as a boy and seeing the wild horses frolicking in the waves. He stopped to watch them, but something caught his eye about a hundred yards out to sea—the gray fin of a shark breaking the surface of the water.

The second week of April brought with it the reality of the formidable challenge before him. Marathon race day loomed less than four weeks away. Training continued without a hitch. The ten-mile runs and ninety-minute rides presented no stress that his body couldn't handle. On Sunday he would embark on the last major workout before the race—the twenty-mile run at slightly slower than race pace. If he made it through that run without any major complications, he would feel confident and ready. Then he would use the final three weeks to taper, cutting his last two Sunday runs down to a fifteen miler and a ten miler. He tried not to think too much about the race. When he did, the nervous anticipation stirred in his stomach. It was much too early to have to manage those kinds of physical discomforts. Race day would be soon enough.

On Sunday morning he contemplated calling the boy to see if he could run the first ten miles of the twenty miler with him. They hadn't run together for over two months, and the old man missed his young friend. He lifted the phone but decided against it. Track season had started and the team had their own training schedule. Besides, the boy probably went to church with his family. Forget it, he thought. You have to do this alone. It was a gray, misty day with temperatures in the mid-fifties. Ideal, really, for a twenty-mile run. He slipped into a short-sleeve t-shirt, medium-length running shorts, and his Saucony Triumphs and headed out the door.

He decided to time himself, hoping to average eight minutes a mile or faster. He hit the start button on his watch and took off. As he ran, he thought about the Great One—Johnny Kelly. I'm sixty-four years old and the Great One ran the Boston Marathon sixty-one times—only three times less than my age. What an unbelievable feat! Back then they didn't have high-tech, supportive shoes. How did he last? He must have had perfect biomechanics. He won the race only twice, but to compete in the race sixty-one times is more impressive than winning six or seven or even ten times. At the age of eighty-four he finished his last Boston. That's twenty years older than me. Certainly, at the age of sixty-four I can finish one marathon, even if tremendous pain besets me. I will endure. I will push to the end. I will try to be worthy of the great Johnny Kelly.

The old man then remembered his junior high days at Central School when Mrs. Woods caught him chewing gum in eighth grade history class. He faced the standard punishment called the Standing Cross: The offender stood in front of the class with arms spread like one being crucified but with palms up. Mrs. Woods placed an Ohio History book in each hand. She stood near the transgressor with a paddle. If he could hold up the books for thirty minutes, he would escape a hard whack with the paddle. If his arms dropped, she would swing the board like a baseball bat. No one had ever lasted thirty minutes, and the crack could always be heard throughout the entire school.

The first five minutes wasn't bad. He watched the second hand make its laps around the clock on the back wall. Then his arms began to ache. He noticed several of the students writing on scraps of paper and crumpling them into small balls. Then they passed the slips of paper over to Michael Burns when Mrs. Woods wasn't watching. He knew they were taking bets. How many minutes would he last? Students wrote their guesses on the paper. At lunchtime Michael would collect a nickel from each kid and give the winnings to the one who made the best guess.

At ten minutes sweat began to drip into his eyes. He blinked several times and noticed Michael unraveling the balls of paper. Michael flashed him the number of fingers for each guess. Someone guessed twelve, another fifteen, another seventeen, but no one guessed over twenty. That made him even more determined. He gritted his teeth and blocked the pain out of his mind. At fifteen minutes his shoulders went numb. At seventeen minutes his face muscles started to twitch.

Mrs. Woods drew close and met his gaze. She was a small woman but stout with a nose like an eagle's beak. She wore wire-rimmed glasses and had wiry salt-and-pepper hair. "You think you're pretty tough, huh, Angelo?"

He didn't respond.

"We'll see. Just remember, though, the longer you last, the harder I hit; unless, of course, you make the full thirty minutes. But no one has ever come close to that."

Twenty minutes passed and his arms trembled. He swallowed and tried to blank the pain out of his mind. The numbness crept down his arms to his elbows. He took slow, deep breaths and focused on the minute hand taking its laps—21 . . . 22 . . . 23. At twenty-five minutes the students buzzed with the realization that they were witnessing an historic effort. Mrs. Woods turned and shouted, "Quiet!" She took the paddle and whacked her desktop. The room became silent, but the stillness intensified the atmosphere of anticipation. At twenty-seven minutes his arms trembled even more noticeably. Sweat had soaked into his gray t-shirt leaving large wet patches under his armpits. He glanced around the room and noticed the kids' amazed expressions. Then their amazement turned into hard-to-conceal elation as the last two minutes ticked away. With thirty seconds to go Michael Burns began a whispered countdown. Despite great fear of Mrs. Woods, several students joined him. To the class's great surprise, Mrs. Woods counted down the last ten seconds with them. Then she reached and removed the books from his hands, and applause broke out. He lowered his arms, walked back to his seat, and sat down. All eyes were upon him.

"Quite a display of endurance, Angelo. I commend you." Mrs. Woods raised her finger and pointed at him. "But I better never catch you chewing gum in my room again."

The bell rang, and the kids gathered around him, moving en masse out the door and toward the cafeteria. When they arrived, Michael Burns collected a nickel from every kid who submitted a guess and presented the handful of coins to Angelo at the lunch table. He counted the money—twenty nickels in all, an even dollar. Everyone slapped him on the back and praised his valiant effort. He felt like a hero from some ancient Greek myth, perhaps Odysseus or Achilles. On his way home from school that day he stopped off at the news stand on Hanover Street and bought five candy bars, three bags of potato chips, and two bottles of pop. He still had one nickel left over, a Buffalo nickel or otherwise known as an Indian Head. He decided to keep it to commemorate the triumph. To this day the nickel rests in the top drawer of his dresser in a small jewelry box that once belonged to his grandmother.

The old man snapped out of his memories and realized he had reached the turnaround point in Warwood. He had covered six and a half miles and felt great. Running back to Martins Ferry would total thirteen. Then he would complete the twenty miler with a seven-mile loop in the country—out Glenns Run and up over Dump Hill. He was astonished at how fast time flew during long runs when his mind was occupied. He glanced at his watch to see if he was on pace: 52:05—spot on.

Of course, he reasoned, time was an invention of man. Someone invented the clock which divided the day into minutes and hours. It was all very mathematical. But why did time go so slowly during the last mile of a 5K race and so quickly on a leisurely run? The math did not change. Each second and minute was still the same length. The old man knew the answer: pain and pleasure. Pleasure made time go quickly and pain slowed it to a snail's pace. The thought disturbed the old man, knowing that marathoners claimed the last six miles of the 26.2 mile race were the most excruciating a runner would ever experience. It was called "hitting the wall." During that phase of the race time must go slower than a turtle wading through molasses, the old man thought.

After a few minutes his mind drifted again to memories of long ago. He recalled his freshmen track teammates and how they would climb the fence at the football stadium on Sunday afternoons and hold their own decathlon. What a blast it was to compete for fun in the high jump, broad jump, hurdles, weights, and sprints. Back then the high jump pit consisted of thick netting filled with chunks of foam rubber. If you landed on a sparsely padded section, boy, it could smart. One day he cleared five feet six inches with a near perfect western roll. His buddies couldn't believe it. They challenged him to do it again, but he couldn't duplicate the feat. It was one of those magical moments in life when the stars aligned and all the pieces fell into place.

After the competition they would grab their fishing poles and head down to the old dam to see who could catch the most carp or catfish. Before they knew it, the sun had set, and the day had slipped away on them. The old man couldn't understand today's kids. They lived in a virtual world of computer graphics. Yes, they played football, baseball, basketball, and hockey all day, but they did it on computer screens using some kind of handheld controller. No wonder most them were overweight and out of shape. When they went out for a real sport, their bodies were traumatized by engaging in actual exercise. Perhaps that was why so many of them ended up injured during the first week of practice.

The old man had to confess he was computer illiterate. To sign up for the Pittsburgh Marathon he had visited his friend, Bruce Pascal, back in late January. Bruce had kept up with the times. He quickly logged on to the website, brought up the registration page, and entered the information and credit card number. It only took a couple minutes. Bruce printed out the confirmation and about six pages of important packet-pickup details and race day instructions for him. The old man hated the idea that his credit card information was now forever on record somewhere in cyberspace. But what could he do? The computer age had overtaken the world.

Suddenly, he realized he was back in Martins Ferry and starting on the final seven-mile loop. He checked his watch: 1:44:15. The pace was almost perfect, and he felt great. With his confidence soaring, he spent the next several miles dreaming about the race. The running magazines all advocated the positive mental approach of envisioning success. This made sense to him. In his mind's eye he pictured himself running smoothly, relaxed, and breathing under control and in rhythm. Then he imagined hitting the wall at the twenty-mile mark. He did not allow it to overpower him. He saw himself gathering his mental focus and pushing through the pain. Finally, in his mind he crossed the finish line to the roar of the crowd.

At the end of Glenn's Run he made a left turn up Dump Hill. Two and a half miles to go, he told himself. One step at a time. You can do this. Rita Marling infiltrated his mind. Sometimes he had to pinch himself to make sure his romantic relationship with her wasn't a fantasy. Why would a beauty like Rita want to date him? With a ten-year age difference and his lack of sophistication, they seemed like an unlikely pair. He wondered if she would want to go up to Pittsburgh with him on the morning of the race.

He had already decided not to stay in a hotel room. On the day before the marathon he would drive up to the David L. Lawrence Convention Center and pick up his packet and then drive home. He didn't mind. He'd sleep much better in his own bed. The race started at seven in the morning. He would leave home at 4 a.m. and get there by 5:30 or at the latest six. He doubted that Rita would want to get up that early and accompany him. Oh well, he thought. It didn't hurt to ask. There was no doubt in his mind that Manny would want to go. Would his parents put up a fuss? The boy would probably pester them until they relented. Wouldn't it be great if both Rita and the boy went? That way they could keep each other company during the race. On the way home he would stop at a restaurant and treat them all to lunch.

By now the old man had run two-thirds of the way up the hill. He had about four hundred yards to go to the top. His legs felt suddenly heavy, and his breathing accelerated. He figured he had covered eighteen miles to this point. Once he made it to the top, finishing would be easy: The last mile and a half was mostly downhill. An odd pain needled the outside of his lower right leg. Oh no, he thought. His mind traveled back in time twenty years to the day he first felt sciatica pain. It started in the exact same spot. Back then he figured it was just a slight strain. He had no idea that the nerve was being pressured by a disc in his back which referred the pain to his lower leg. He had been training for his first marathon.

He kept putting one foot in front of the other, waiting to see if the pain would increase. At any moment he expected it to shoot up his hamstring and into his right buttocks. If it did, he would immediately stop. Refusing to stop was his big mistake twenty years ago. His stubbornness resulted in severe damage to the sciatic nerve which caused temporary paralysis and total loss of feeling. Because of the lack of proper nerve conduction in his leg, he had torn several muscles and injured tendons. The injury lasted an agonizing eight years. The body repairs nerves very slowly.

At the top of the hill the pain disappeared. Perhaps he was being overly fearful. Runners put up with constant aches and discomforts. This was just one of the thousands of pains that came knocking on his body over the years. Often they go away. Sometimes they come back.

"You worry too much, old man," he said aloud.

There was good pain and bad pain. The right amount of training created good pain which damaged the muscles slightly. In response, the body repaired the fibers to be even stronger than before. Overtraining created bad pain which did too much damage for the body to reasonably repair within a day or two. Serious injuries resulted. The insightful runner knew how much training his body could take before it would break down. As he neared the bottom of the hill, he focused on the outside of the lower right leg. The pain still had not returned. It was only a temporary discomfort, he thought. Nothing unusual. It knocked on the door and then went away.

"Don't come back. You're not welcome." He glanced around to see if anyone heard him talking to himself. What the hell, he thought. They would just say I'm a crazy old man.

By the time he rounded the corner of Center Street and First Street, exhaustion weighed upon him like a heavy coat on a warm spring day. He didn't mind; a twenty -mile run should totally deplete his energy reserves, tiring him completely. He checked his watch: two hours and thirty-five minutes. Excellent! He was slightly ahead of pace. As he covered the last few hundred yards to his house, he felt confident that he was ready to run a marathon. The hard work had been deposited in the training bank. Now he needed to allow his body to fully recover in the next three weeks but still maintain the conditioning level he had achieved. Then, on race day, it would come time to withdraw all the hard work he had invested.

On the first Saturday in May, the old man drove into the country to pick up Rita Marling. To his great surprise, not only did she want to accompany him on race day but also insisted on riding to the convention center with him to pick up his packet the day before. She professed that she loved the city of Pittsburgh and prided herself as a dedicated fan of the Steelers, Pirates, and Penguins. The old man didn't care that much about professional sports like he did when he was younger. His heroes didn't need helmets or shin guards or athletic cups. They wore the lightest of clothing and shoes. No field or arena or boundary confined them, but rather they ran freely for miles and miles pushing themselves to the limit of human endurance. To the old man, these were true heroes—Rodgers, Beardsley, Shorter, de Castela, Higdon, Hill, Jones, Salazar, and of course, the Great One, Johnny Kelly.

When he had told her about the marathon expo with all its vendors, stands, clothing, shoes, and information booths, she became doubly excited. She loved to shop and hoped to get some good deals on athletic apparel. Her dancing had kept her in good shape, and the old man had no doubt that she would look good in an Adidas or Nike running outfit.

As they drove up the Penn Lincoln Highway to the top of the hill before the long descent to the Fort Pitt Tunnel, Rita asked, "Do all the runners have to come up the day before the race to pick up their packets?"

"Yes. With over 25,000 entrants it would be impossible to manage the crowd on the morning of the race."

"I see. I'm amazed that so many people want to torture themselves for twenty-six miles."

"Only about six thousand run the full marathon. The rest run the half."

When they entered the tunnel, Rita asked, "Do you know your way around downtown Pittsburgh?"

"It's not my favorite place to drive."

"I come up a few times a year. I can help you get to where you're going. You know, we should have stayed in a hotel up here tonight."

The old man shot a quick glance her way. "You would have stayed in a hotel room with me?"

"Sure. Why not?"

"I didn't want to be presumptuous, but now I wish I would have known that."

Rita flashed her wide smile. "I didn't say I'd do the wild thing with you."

The old man chuckled. "The wild thing? I'd never do that the night before a marathon. It weakens the legs."

Rita slugged his shoulder. "Of course you wouldn't. The marathon comes before everything, even making love to a gorgeous woman. At least I can say one thing for you."

"What's that?"

"Your dedication to running takes precedence over natural human behavior."

The old man took that as a high compliment.

The David L. Lawrence Convention Center wasn't hard to find. After making it through the tunnel, they crossed the Fort Pitt Bridge and took the Liberty Avenue exit. Traffic moved slowly and the stoplights seemed to last forever. Get used to it, the old man thought. This is the big city. At Ninth Street, Rita told him to make a left and find a reasonably priced parking garage. At the next corner the old man turned right on Penn Avenue and spotted a sign that said PARKING - $6.00. He turned into the garage and weaved up through the cavernous structure about six floors until he found an empty space. As they walked to the elevator, Rita reached and took his hand. This tickled him. With the comment about staying the night in a hotel room together and the hand holding, he wondered if he had successfully reeled in Miss Marling's heart.

The convention center overlooked the river, and to the old man, the white steel framework resembled the skeleton of a giant ship under construction. Once inside they descended to the lowest floor where the expo was located. Just outside of the entrance doors stood a large yellow sign with black stenciled lettering at the top: WHAT'S HARDER THAN STEEL? Then came a silhouette of a bridge and below it the answer to the question in white stenciled lettering: THE LAST SIX MILES. This sent a chill through the old man as he recalled the pain on the side of his lower leg from three weeks ago. He shook his head to get rid of the negative thought.

The room appeared as big as a football field with high ceilings. Rows upon rows of popup tents and tables with myriad colors of flags, banners, and signs took up the entire area. The vendors peddled everything related to running: shoes, socks, apparel, jewelry, vitamin supplements, gel packs, massage and medical services, orthotic inserts, equipment bags, books, sports creams, nutrition bars, and on and on. Through the spectacle of wares, advertising, and shuffling people, the old man spotted a sign directing runners to the packet pickup area toward the back.

"I've got to go this way to get my packet."

"That's fine," Rita said. "I'm going to do some shopping. Look at all these vendors!"

"How will I find you?"

Rita swiveled her head until she spied something. "I see a lot of clothing and shoes in that direction. "I'll hang out over there until you're finished."

The old man nodded and headed in the direction of the queues of people waiting to get their packets. The marathon lines were shorter than the half marathon lines. He found his particular alphabetical index, Q through T, and fell in at the end. A thin man with long, sandy-brown hair and a Roman nose stood in front of him tapping his foot. The old man guessed the stranger to be in his mid-forties.

The long-haired guy faced him. "Are you ready for tomorrow?"

"I hope so," the old man said.

"We never know, do we?"

"Nothing is guaranteed."

"What kind of time are you shooting for?"

The old man scratched his chin. "I want to run under three hours and fifty-five minutes in order to qualify for Boston, but I think I can make a stab at 3:30."

"How old are you?"

"Sixty-four."

"That's quite fast for your age. I'm forty-five. My qualifying standard is three hours and twenty-five minutes. It will be difficult for me. I've run ten marathons but have never qualified for Boston."

"Maybe tomorrow will be your day. Do you have a race plan?"

The long-haired man nodded. "I want to run negative spits. Average 7:55 the first thirteen miles and then try to go faster the second half. Usually, I go out too fast and die."

"Good plan. I hope to go eight-minute miles the whole way. Maybe I'll see you out there."

The man extended his hand. "I'm Jan Steinberg."

The old man shook his hand. "Angelo Santiago."

"Good luck, Angelo. Let's run like wildebeests tomorrow."

"Or better yet, like Kenyans."

The line moved quickly, and the old man received his number, a complementary carrying bag, and a ticket to pick up his commemorative marathon t-shirt. He eyed his number—1371. Why did thirteen have to appear on his race number? Bad luck, I suppose, he told himself. Quit being a superstitious old fool. If you believe in bad luck, it will surely come your way. Think positive.

He was a true believer in the mind's influence on the body. He once had a friend who went to see a fortune teller. The psychic predicted the day his friend would die. From that day on his buddy was never the same. That date loitered at the back of his mind casting a negative shadow on his life's path. When the day finally came and went without incident, it was too late. The damage had already been done. His friend had been conditioned to trudge along on the negative side of life. To manage his imagined stress, he ate and drank too much and finally died of a heart attack at the age of fifty-nine, almost exactly one year after the fortune teller's prediction.

The old man picked up his shirt at a nearby table. It was one of those new mirco-fiber shirts, yellow with a neat image of the silhouette of three runners at the base of a triangle and a suspension bridge above them. Because the Allegheny and Monongahela converged to form the Ohio River near the middle of town,

Pittsburgh became known as the City of Bridges. The old man wondered how many bridges the competitors would cross during the race. He enjoyed running across bridges. They offered the promise of something new—the other side. It occurred to him that running this marathon was a bridge to something new. He reminded himself to appreciate the atmosphere created by the bridges, the people, and town itself during the race. Stop and smell the roses, he told himself. Well, maybe not stop, but at least take it all in. At the pace he hoped to run, he should feel comfortable most of the way and able to enjoy his surroundings. However, the last six miles would require every ounce of his focus. Once he hit the wall, smelling roses would be very difficult.

He headed back in the direction where Rita waited. Down one row he noticed an incredible deal on running socks. He had to stop. Over the years he had discovered how much he preferred quality running socks to the generic kind one buys at a department store. These were Saucony socks, the same company that manufactured his favorite shoes, and the price was incredible—three pair for five dollars. He bought thirty pair. The guy at the register gave him an odd look, but he didn't care. When would he find a deal like this again? Maybe never.

Nearby he noticed another stand selling GU Gel Packs. He had read about these energy boosters many times in the running magazines. Because he raced mostly 5Ks, he never had the opportunity to use them. Now is the time, he thought. Perhaps ingesting the gooey, calorie-loaded substance during the race would provide much needed energy for the final six miles. He looked over the flavors and picked up three packs—chocolate, blackberry, and a strawberry-banana. He remembered reading instructions from one particular article about pinning the packs to your shorts. He made a mental note to toss some extra safety pins into his running bag that evening when he arrived home.

Finally, he made it back to the corner where Rita said she would be waiting. He glanced down each row but didn't see her. He decided to walk up and down the rows in case she was tucked behind someone or something that blocked her from his view. No Rita. Maybe she got bored and wandered off in another direction, he thought. He walked toward the opposite corner inspecting the aisles as he passed. What was she wearing? He closed his eyes to remember. Ah . . . yes—a bright pink top with capri jeans.

Finally, he spotted her standing next to a rack of shoes and talking to some man. As he drew closer he recognized the guy—Coach Silvers. He was wearing a black ball cap and black polo shirt with a white shark logo on the breast. As he neared he could pick up snippets of their conversation. They were talking about dancing. Silvers noticed him approaching and waved.

"Angelo, great to see you."

"How are you doing, Coach?" He extended his hand.

Silvers shook it and said, "Couldn't be better. And you?"

"Can't complain."

"Ready for the big day?"

"I hope so." The old man hesitated, wondering if he should ask the question, but then he proceeded. "Did you rest up, or are you training through this one?"

Silvers smiled, but his eyes remained cold and lifeless. "Very funny. I'm well rested. I take the marathon seriously. I hope to qualify for my sixth Boston tomorrow. How many times have you qualified?"

The old man felt the verbal dagger pierce him. "You are way ahead of me in that department."

"I'm sorry. Now I remember. This is your first marathon, right?"

"Right."

"And you have potential sciatica problems."

"Right again, but no runner is exempt from catastrophe in a marathon."

Rita patted the old man's shoulder. "Angelo tells me he believes he can beat you."

Silvers raised his eyebrows. "Really?"

The old man shook his head. "Rita, why did you mention that?"

Her mouth dropped open. "You did tell me that."

"That's okay," Silvers said. "I believe I'm gonna kick your ass tomorrow." He smiled again, the cold, lifeless eyes piercing through the old man. Silvers raised his hand. "I'm just kidding around. It's my competitive nature coming out."

"I've got good advice for both of us. Believing is one thing, but doing is another."

"Well said." Silvers glanced at his watch and then eyed Rita. "I'm glad I ran into you, but I'm meeting some friends for dinner, so I've got to get back to my hotel."

Rita leaned and gave him a quick pat on the shoulder. "Good luck tomorrow, Jack."

"Thanks, and remember if you ever need a dance partner, keep me in mind."

"I will."

Silvers nodded toward him. "See you at the starting line."

The old man nodded back and thought, yes, and I will do my damnedest to leave you in my dust.

𓀀𓀀𓀀𓀀𓀀

He was running barefoot along the beach with the wild horses galloping by his side when the alarm went off at three o'clock in the morning. The loud beeps startled his heart, and he could feel the beating up into his throat. I must move quickly, the old man thought. I will be at the starting line in four hours. He reached and pressed the switch on the light atop his nightstand, sat up, swung his legs over the bed, and planted his feet on the floor. He glanced up to see his racing outfit neatly laid over the back of a wooden chair next to the bed. On the seat of the chair sat his Saucony Fastwitch racing flats with the new socks he had purchased at the expo the day before tucked into the openings.

Adrenaline charged through him, and he jumped to his feet. Take it easy, he told himself. It's too early to be this nervous. He quickly funneled into his yellow tank top and stepped into black trunks, the very short ones worn by most serious competitors. He had already pinned his number to his racing top and the three gel packs to his shorts. The local weatherman had predicted a morning low of fifty-five degrees, a temperature the old man considered perfect for his body type. He pulled an old black long-sleeve t-shirt over his racing top. This would keep him warm at the starting line. He would peel it off and toss it to the side just before the race started. Next he slipped on his socks and racing flats, making sure to double knot his shoestrings. He glanced at the alarm clock: 3:05. He hurried downstairs to eat breakfast—two toaster waffles, a glass of orange juice, and a large cup of coffee. By 3:30 he was out the door.

🏃🏃🏃🏃🏃

His stomach gurgled as he drove to the boy's house. He feared he had gobbled his breakfast down too quickly. He stopped along the curb and beeped the horn. A minute went by. What's taking him so long? Finally, the front light brightened the porch and the boy charged out of the house. He threw open the car door and jumped into the front seat.

"Sorry, I had to go to the bathroom. Number two." the boy said.

The old man hit the gas and sped down the street. "That's okay. I will have to go too sooner or later. I hope sooner. I want my system to empty out before the race starts."

"There's nothing worse than having to go during the race."

"Amen to that."

"How are you feeling?"

"Good."

"I have much confidence in you."

"Thanks. I've done everything I'm supposed to do. I've put in the miles. I did the long runs. Every other day I cross trained on the bike. Now I just have one more thing to do."

"What's that?"

"Run a good race."

"You will," the boy said, nodding. "I know you will."

The old man stopped at the red light on Hanover Street and glanced at the boy. "Your confidence cheers me up, but I must face a very sobering fact."

The boy met his gaze. "What fact?"

"No one can run this race for me. It's something I must do alone."

"I understand," the boy said. "Only you can reach deep inside of yourself."

"That's right, Manny. I am the only one who can reach deep inside and withdraw what I have invested."

Rita was waiting on her porch when the old man pulled into her driveway. She rushed to the car, and the boy swung open the door, stepped out, and held the door for her while she slid into the front seat. Manny yanked open the back door and climbed in. The old man checked his watch—3:55. From Rita's house in the country it would take about an hour and a half to get to downtown Pittsburgh. Plenty of time, the old man thought, just in case they run in to some unforeseen traffic delay.

"I can't remember the last time I got up this early," Rita said.

"It will be dark for at least two more hours, "the old man said.

Rita put her hand on his knee. "Are you nervous?"

"I'm excited, but I want to remain as calm as possible. I don't want to burn unnecessary calories from being too anxious."

"Are you worried about Jack Silvers?"

"Jack Silvers?" the boy interrupted. "Do you mean Coach Silvers?"

"Yes."

"Why would Angelo worry about him?"

Rita turned and eyed Manny. "They seem to have a rivalry. The way they talked yesterday, I could feel the testosterone broiling in the air between them."

The boy laughed. "I like Coach Silvers, but Angelo will have no problem cleaning his clock."

"I don't know if I want to clean his clock," the old man said. Then he thought, I'd like to step on it, crush it, and then hand the pieces to him.

"Please," Rita said. "I can tell when two men want to tangle. You were like young lions fighting over mating rights."

The old man's voice raised an octave: "Mating rights for who? I think you are exaggerating. Coach Silvers and I are very competitive. We'll step up to the starting line today and do our best to beat each other."

Rita raised her hands. "Okay. No need to get your hackles up. May the best man win."

The old man took a deep breath and blew it out. "My hackles are fine. I have no control over Jack Silvers and how fast he runs. I'll do my best. That's all I can do." They drove in silence for a while, and the old man steamed, thinking how he really wanted to clean Jack Silvers' clock. Then he felt guilty for wanting to humble another man to impress a woman or to show he is the better man. He needed to worry about his own race and not let a competitor interfere with his strategy. Silvers had meant for his comments to irritate him. The marathon gave the old man enough of a mental challenge without having to deal with the mind games of a rival.

Halfway to Pittsburgh he pulled off at a rest stop along Interstate 70. All three of them headed to the restroom. The old man had a great bowel movement. This made him feel a lot better. He wanted to empty himself as much as possible just in case the lines at the port-a-potties were long. In a race with 25,000 participants, the last place he wanted to be was standing in line to relieve himself minutes before the start of the race. By the time he got back to the car, Rita and Manny were sitting inside the vehicle.

He started the engine, backed out, and zoomed onto the on ramp.

"Feeling any better?" Rita asked.

"Much better."

"It took you a while. You must have deposited a few bricks back there," she said.

The old man chuckled. "Enough to build a house."

Manny laughed. "That's quite a production."

The rest of the way the mood lightened. They talked about the best places to watch the race, what to do during the long wait when the runners were circling the city and the plans for after the race. The boy and Rita decided they would find a good restaurant to eat breakfast, hopefully not far from the finish line. The old man mentioned that he would like to treat them to lunch on the way home. Before they knew it they were driving up the final hill before the descent to the Fort Pitt Tunnel. Halfway down the hill, the traffic backed up. Oh no, the old man thought. This must be race traffic. He checked his watch: 5:30. Who else would be coming into downtown Pittsburgh this early? In ninety minutes the gun would go off.

It took almost forty-five minutes to drive the mile and a half from midway down the hill, through the Fort Pitt Tunnel, across the bridge, and onto Liberty Avenue. The old man finally found a parking garage with empty spaces about six blocks from the starting line. By the time he turned off the car he felt incredibly tense.

"It's 6:25," the old man said. "I've got to get over to the starting line and get a spot in the front of my corral."

"Get going," Rita said. "Don't wait for us. We're only about ten or fifteen minutes from the start."

"You don't mind me leaving you?"

"Of course not. Manny is with me, and I'm a big girl. I know my way around here."

"Thanks. Hopefully, I'll see you at the start."

"Good luck, Angelo," the boy said. "I know you will run like a champion."

"Come here," Rita said. "Give me a good luck kiss before you take off."

The old man leaned toward her, and she clasped his face with her hands, drew him near, and kissed him on the lips, a wet, warm kiss.

Now he felt supercharged. He climbed out of the car and bolted toward the stairwell. Calm down, he told himself. But he couldn't help sensing the intensity of that kiss. Was he falling in love? At the stairs he noticed a large "3" painted on the wall. A group of people waited in front of an elevator. The steps would be faster. He double-timed it down three flights and exited the garage onto a downtown street. The sky had lightened in the east creating a pale backdrop against the tall, dark buildings. The old man looked around to gain his bearings. He noticed most of the people, many of them wearing running outfits, heading west. "That's the direction I want to go," he said aloud.

It didn't take him long to jog the six blocks to the starting line. It served as his warm up. He heard rock music blaring and an announcer cutting in intermittently instructing runners to enter the correct corral, which was indicated on their bib number. He had submitted a time of 3:40 and was assigned to corral B. To his right on the corner of Stanwix Street and Liberty Avenue he noticed a McDonalds. The sidewalks were crowded, and a fence composed of bright orange plastic vinyl separated the sidewalk from the street. Liberty Avenue was filled with runners who had already entered their corral. In the middle of the street a volunteer stood with a large poster board sign he held high on a pole with a large letter "C" on it. Corral B must be another block away, he reasoned.

It took him several minutes, but he finally weaved in and out of the crowd along the sidewalk and made his way to the corral entrance on Sixth Street. He did not want to get caught at the back of the corral, so he squeezed through clusters of runners who talked nervously or tried to stretch in the limited space. Patiently he worked his way to the front. It was definitely more crowded toward the front which made it almost impossible to stretch. He checked his watch: 6:45. Fifteen minutes and the race would start. A shot of adrenaline rushed through him, and he took a deep breath in an effort to calm himself.

"Angelo," an unfamiliar voice called.

He turned to see the long-haired man he had met while waiting in line to get his packet the day before. He tried to remember his name. Was it Jan? Yes, that was it. "How are you doing, Jan?"

"Hanging in there like a loose tooth. You?"

"Maybe a little nervous."

"Like a lamb at Passover I bet."

"We're certainly packed in here like sheep in a pen."

"It'll be crowded for the first few miles. Eventually we'll get some breathing room. Nice thing about a race this big, it never gets lonely."

"Are you sticking with your race plan—7:55 miles for the first 13 miles?" The old man asked.

"Definitely. Then I'll pick up the pace. Try to run 7:45s the rest of the way."

"I'd like to run with you for the first half of the race, if you don't mind."

"Sure. Be nice to have the company. See the guy at the back of Corral A holding up the sign?"

The old man stood on his toes to get a better look. "The sign that says 3:20?"

"Yeah. He's the pacesetter. That group should slowly pull away from us in the first mile. Behind us is the 3:30 group. If they pass us, you know we're running too slow."

"I might drop back with them after the first thirteen miles. That's the time I want to hit."

Jan bobbed his head. "That'd be great for your age. Twenty-five minutes ahead of Boston qualifying time."

"Well . . ." The old man shook his head. "That's my reach-for-the-stars goal. I'll be satisfied if I qualify for Boston."

"Hey! Angelo!"

From behind, the old man heard the voice of Jack Silvers. He turned and spotted him. "Hi, Coach."

Silvers wore a black running cap with a white shark logo on it and a matching racing top. "I thought we might be in the same corral."

They shook hands and the old man introduced him to Jan. After discussing pace and time goals, Silvers said, "You boys will be ahead of me. I plan to run 8:10s the whole way. Steady pace is the key to qualifying for Boston. If I were you, Angelo, I'd stick with me. Going out with Jan might be a critical error."

The old man shook his head. "I think I can handle it."

Silvers chuckled. "Don't complain then if I pass you at twenty miles and say, 'I told you so.'"

The old man kept his mouth shut. He wanted to say: You have a snowball's chance in hell of beating me. But if you do, I wouldn't complain or make an excuse. Too many words and too much ego, the old man thought. I can't let my pride direct my tongue.

The announcer bellowed, "Five minutes until race time!"

I've got to get rid of this long sleeve t-shirt, the old man thought. He peeled it off and tossed it into the crowd of spectators beyond the plastic fence. He didn't feel cold at all because of the body heat of the competitors around him. He shook out his arms and legs. Then he reached down and pulled off one of the foil gel packs from his shorts, tore off the top, and sucked it down. Chocolate. Not bad at all. He planned on eating one at eight miles and one at sixteen. Of course, on the run it will be much more difficult, and he will probably need to get a cup of water from a race volunteer to help wash it down.

He glanced behind him and saw a sea of runners filling the avenue and disappearing around a turn. The sky had turned pale blue and the tops of the skyscrapers caught the rays of the sun. An energy, like electricity, buzzed through the runners as they waited for the last few minutes to pass. They were united in this unique sense of elation, taking on an incredible challenge together. The old man sucked in a deep breath and blew it out, closed his eyes, said a quick prayer, and then shook out his hands and feet out again. The running test of his life was about to begin.

"One minute!" The announcer chimed.

The old man bounced on his toes a couple times like a boxer before the fight. He checked his watch to make sure it was in chronograph mode and reset to zero. He steadied himself, placing his right leg in front of his left and crouching slightly. Don't start your watch at the gun, he reminded himself. Wait until you cross the starting line a block from here. He knew the automatic timing strip in his bib number would start his individual time when he passed over the sensing device. The technology is amazing, he thought, but still, I trust my own watch more.

"Here we go!" the announcer said. "Ten! Nine! Eight! Seven! Six! Five! Four! Three! Two! One!" A loud boom rumbled down the street from about a block away. Slowly but steadily, the runners moved like a herd of cattle toward the starting line. Ahead, the old man could see the yellow arch that stretched from one side of the avenue to the other with both the Dick's Sporting Goods and Pittsburgh Marathon logos across the top of it. As he passed under the arch, he started his watch.

His intuitive pacing sense told him they were running too slow. There wasn't much he could do about it because of the crowd. If he tried to cut through, he would risk tripping someone or perhaps falling himself.

He glanced up at Jan, who was running beside him and tapped his watch.

"I know," Jan said. "It'll be like this for the first mile. Then we can settle into the right pace."

I need to be patient, the old man thought. Smell the roses. He panned the scene in front of him. Above the multitude of runners the buildings rose up ten to twelve stories high, making the road seem like a deep channel through which they were passing. He noticed one building on the right taller than most, maybe twenty stories high. The sunshine brightened the sign on the very top of the building: Duquesne Light. He was amazed at the number of trees along the street considering he was running through a downtown metropolis. Pittsburgh, once a smoggy, dust-covered steel and coal town, was in the middle of a renaissance. The restored buildings and clean surroundings impressed the old man.

The pace picked up, making him less anxious. They ran under a couple of wide overpasses which doused the brightening day, and in the sudden darkness he heard vehicles rumbling above him. Re-entering the sunlight, he noticed the absence of tall buildings, replaced by a long cement wall to his right and two-story warehouses on his left. He heard country music in the distance and guessed they were coming up on one of the many live bands providing entertainment for the runners.

Jan pointed to the left. "There's the clock for the one mile split."

The old man focused on the large digital readout: 9:10. Way too slow! Then he checked his watch and noticed it was about one minute behind the race clock. Noting the adjustment due to starting about a minute behind the leaders, he breathed a sigh of relief. They were only about fifteen seconds behind pace.

During the second mile the density of the crowd thinned and they picked up their pace. With a little more room to run, the old man could focus on form. He wanted to run as efficiently as possible. The top marathoners in the world ran effortlessly with no wasted motion. They did not over stride or under stride. By watching their relaxed gait, an observer would never guess they were hitting 4:45 per mile pace. The old man knew he ran much slower but everything was relative. By focusing on good form and relaxation he could take the efficiency factor up a few notches. Over twenty-six miles this could make a big difference.

At Twenty-Ninth Street they made a left turn and then another quick left down Penn Avenue, heading back in the direction of the start. On the corner he noticed an old one-story brick building with a sign above the door that said Art's Tavern. It resembled one of the many little hometown bars you could find in Martins Ferry or Wheeling. I could drink a beer right now, he told himself, but that would be a mistake. Drinking alcohol dehydrates the body. He wondered if he should be drinking water at each water stop. There were so many, one nearly every mile. Just ahead he saw the two mile sign. He checked his watch when they went by: 16:01. They were only ten seconds behind pace.

"We're doing good," Jan said.

"It feels like we're jogging."

"Don't let these early miles fool you. We're still running on adrenaline."

"I know. It just seems so easy right now."

"You won't be saying that two hours from now."

He knew Jan was right. Running eight-minute miles for the first half of the race shouldn't be that stressful. The challenge will be keeping that pace for the second half. About a mile away he could see the skyscrapers looming above the two-story structures in the neighborhood immediately ahead of him. Most of these taller buildings were located near the confluence of the Monongahela River and Allegheny River which formed the mouth of the Ohio River. The area was known as the Golden Triangle, near where the race started. The old man tried to recall the race route. Would they be passing by the start again? Yes, at some point they would come near the start again, but he couldn't remember exactly when. He'd keep his eye on the tall buildings. He wanted to make sure he spotted Manny and Rita and waved to them when he passed.

As the blocks went by he noticed the number of spectators increasing. To his right he saw a huge mural painted on the side of a building. It was a colorful city scene of brick streets and storefronts. He waved at the people standing in front of the building as they clapped and cheered. Then the runners entered the famous Strip District. Abandoned warehouses from the old manufacturing days had been renovated into specialty shops, produce stores, nightclubs, bars, and restaurants. People crowded the sidewalks here, and the colorful awnings, signs, and merchandise displays gave the neighborhood a real ethnic flavor. On one corner a group of musicians with tambourines and guitars played a lively Spanish song. Many of the spectators were dancing and clapping.

Up ahead he could see the runners making a right turn. They were still at least ten blocks from the start. That answered the old man's question. The race route didn't go directly back to the start. Once he made the turn he could see they were headed toward a bridge, the Sixteenth Street Bridge, according to a sign that pointed in that direction. He could see two stone towers and the yellow framework several hundred yards away. As they neared the bridge, he noticed the three-mile marker. He checked his watch: 23:50—only a few seconds off pace. Good, he thought. They were moving up gradually, not forcing themselves to catch up at all.

As they crossed over the Allegheny River, the old man glanced to his left and noticed the downtown skyscrapers and several more bridges before the river disappeared around the bend.

"How many bridges will we cross?" the old man asked.

"Quite a few," Jan said. "Five or six I think. It's one of my favorite things about this race."

"Life is about crossing bridges."

"What do you mean?"

"Your goal today is to qualify for Boston, right?"

"Right."

"That's a bridge you want to cross."

"For sure," Jan said. "But I've tried many times and haven't made it across yet."

"But you're a man of hope."

"Why do you say that?"

"Because you keep trying. You haven't given up."

"Are you a man of hope too?"

"Of course. Here I am sixty-four years old with a history of sciatica trying to run my first marathon. Either I am a man of hope or I'm crazy. What do you think?"

Jan smiled. "I'd say both."

Several hundred yards after crossing the bridge, they made a left and passed under an interstate highway. Probably Interstate 279, the old man figured. Not long after that, he heard someone yelling his name. He eyed the crowd and spotted Manny waving his arms.

Standing next to him, Rita cupped her hands and hollered, "Go, Angelo!"

He smiled, waved, and rounded the corner, turning left again. Energy shot through him as he remembered Rita's kiss. Settle down now, he told himself. You have a long way to go and there will be many more kisses. Manny and Rita must have walked about a mile from the starting line to get to that corner. The old man tried to recall the map. He felt confident the race route passed near that spot again. It would be the last opportunity for the boy and Rita to cheer for him before the course led the runners east for about ten miles and then turned back toward the Golden Triangle.

They ran under another interstate overpass and went by the four-mile marker: 41:40. Right on target. To the old man the pace still seemed relaxing and easy. Ahead he spied another yellow bridge. Did they paint all their bridges yellow? The tall buildings rose up on the other side of the river in the downtown section where the race had started. The bridge arched slightly with huge cables suspending it. The old man drew in deeper breaths as he took on the minor incline to the middle of the span. Glancing to his left he noticed the white framework and expansive sloped roof of the David L. Lawrence Convention Center. The view was quite spectacular with the morning sun reflecting off the building's windows and glistening on the surface of the river.

They made an immediate right after crossing the bridge and ran along a tree-lined street for a couple hundred yards. Then they turned onto the Seventh Street Bridge to re-cross the river. This bridge appeared to be the twin of the last bridge, yellow with thick steel supports reaching down to suspend it above the water. Looking to his left, he saw another similar bridge—triplets. Then it occurred to him: that one must be the Roberto Clemente Bridge. He knew this because he spotted PNC Park just beyond the span along the opposite shore.

Clemente was a tremendous ball player when the old man was a teenager. The all-star had a huge heart, both as a player and a humanitarian. Back in those days the Pirates were a great team, and the old man followed them. Clemente was the greatest of the great, winning golden gloves, batting titles, and leading his team to two World Series Championships.

But because his heart was so big, baseball could not contain it. In the off season he would fly baseball equipment and food to the needy around the world. On a trip to Nicaragua to aid earthquake victims, his plane fell from the sky. He died in his prime, a true hero. The old man often wondered if dying like Clemente was better than dying at the age of ninety in a nursing home with tubes inserted into every hole of the body. He would much prefer Clemente's death. To him, being kept alive by machines wasn't living. This was living: running across the Seventh Street Bridge, legs turning over, arms swinging, lungs breathing. This was life: taking on the challenge of running a marathon—a difficult bridge to cross. He wondered if his heart would be as big as Clemente's when it came to finishing this race.

After crossing the Seventh Street Bridge, the old man kept his eyes peeled for Manny and Rita. He was certain they would be walking in his direction. They would want to head back to the downtown area near the finish and find a good place to eat breakfast. Then he spotted them on the right walking along the sidewalk next to a large parking lot. They both waved their hands above their heads.

"Great job, Angelo!" Manny yelled.

"What happened to Jack Silvers?" Rita hollered. "He's almost two minutes behind you."

"He can't keep up," the old man called back. He chuckled out loud and wondered if Rita was impressed. Silvers was a younger man by ten years and so full of himself. Certainly, Rita saw through the coach's façade. But the old man had to admit that Silvers was a good looking man and liked to dance—two attributes Rita favored.

"Is that your wife?" Jan asked.

"No. She's my girlfriend."

"Quite a beauty."

"I agree. I'm a lucky man."

"Isn't Jack Silvers the guy you introduced me to at the starting line?"

"Yes."

"He seemed a little arrogant. One of those know-it-all kinda guys."

"You and I think alike. But he has accomplished something that we haven't."

"What's that?"

"He has run Boston."

"Oh . . ." Jan kept quiet for about half a minute and then he said, "We'll just have to do something about that. No. Two things."

"Two things?"

"Yeah. Qualify for Boston and kick his ass doing it."

They ran under another interstate overpass, the darkness of its shadow now very noticeable in the morning's bright sunlight. It was still cool out, probably in the high fifties, but the old man knew it would warm up quickly once the sun climbed higher into the sky. He hoped the temperature would not rise above sixty-five before he finished. Most runners do much better in reasonably cool air. Heat can be a killer of dreams and marathon goals. They passed the five-mile mark slightly under pace: 39:32. Twenty-one miles to go and I feel incredibly good, the old man thought. If it doesn't get too warm, I might be able to break 3:30. I wonder how many sixty-year olds are ahead of me. To win my age group would be a glorious accomplishment. Don't get carried away with dreams of glory, he told himself. You are a long way from success—twenty-one miles to be exact. Keep humble, you old fool.

During the next mile they ran along East Commons, turned on North Commons, and again on West Commons, the streets creating a large square where several apartment buildings were located. The old man could see the tall downtown skyscrapers again, but then the runners made a right on Ridge Avenue, and he knew they wouldn't head back into the downtown area again until the final mile. They entered a neighborhood with rows of redbrick townhouses. The old man guessed they had been built in the early 1900's but were still in good shape. They reminded him of the Victorian-style houses at the north end of Wheeling. So far the course had been fairly flat, but he could see sizable hills, the Allegheny Mountain foothills, in the distance. He knew the hills had to be across the Ohio River. They ran past the six-mile marker, and he checked his watch: 47:25—five seconds under pace!

After passing through the redbrick neighborhood, they came to the West End Bridge. This bridge was larger and wider than the others but still painted yellow with huge coil cables dropping down from its expansive arched framework. The old man glanced to his left at the mouth of the Ohio River. I could jump in and swim seventy miles, crawl up on shore, and walk a block to my house, he thought. That made him chuckle. He definitely wasn't a tri-athlete. He'd rather take his chances running the marathon. So far he had had good luck. Knock on wood. But there was no wood nearby, just steel rails, cables, and cement bridge roadway beneath his feet.

At the end of the bridge they made a right and then a quick left under an overpass. It seemed to the old man they were running under major roadways at almost every mile. A few hundred yards later they passed the seven-mile mark, still a few seconds ahead of pace. Now they were running through a working-class neighborhood with lots of old houses and a few small churches, very similar to the streets of Martins Ferry or Bellaire. After several blocks they made a left and then another quick left back in the direction of the river. It occurred to the old man that the eight-mile marker was about a half mile away. He glanced down and saw the remaining two GU Gel Packs. This would be interesting, he thought, trying to suck down this energy goo while running better than an eight-minute per mile pace.

"Did you bring gel packs with you?" the old man asked.

"Yeah." Jan patted his race shirt. "Got special compartments in this shirt to carry them. It's one of those dry-fit jerseys designed for long races."

"If I ever run another marathon, I'll have to get me one."

"They're nice. I saw that you have a couple gel packs pinned to your trunks. Are you about ready to take one?"

"Yes. Any hints? I've never tried this before."

"It's not easy. When we see the next water stop, open one up. Then grab a glass of water and wet your throat. Down the gel pack as best you can and grab another glass of water. That'll help wash it down."

"Makes sense."

"There should be a water stop near the eight mile mark."

Running along Route 837, they came up on the next water stop almost directly across the river from the Golden Triangle. The old man could see the spout of the large fountain at the apex of the triangle where the three rivers met. He reached down and yanked one of the gel packs off the pin and tore off the top of it. He drifted to the right and caught the eyes of a kid dressed in yellow and black and holding up a Styrofoam cup. He pointed at the boy, and the kid nodded. As he went by he snatched the cup and swallowed the water. Half of it spilled out the sides of his mouth. Then he sucked on the end of the gel pack—strawberry-banana. After a couple of gulps he coughed and caught his breath. Then he ran his thumb and finger up the foil pack to empty the rest into his mouth. Holding his breath, he swallowed it down. Not too bad. He still had time to reach out and grab another cup of water off of a middle aged lady wearing sunglasses. After a couple of drinks, he tossed the cup and empty pack to the ground. Not perfect but effective. Hopefully, the effort would pay dividends in the last half of the race.

The next three miles traveled along the river on the south side of Pittsburgh. A lot of trees overhung the road and the Allegheny foothills rose steeply up on the right. They passed Station square, a historical railroad complex that had been turned into a popular nightspot with restaurants bars and specialty shops. The old man knew if they ran another five or ten miles along 837 they would pass by Kennywood Park, the city's popular amusement park with its legendary wooden roller coasters. But right after mile eleven they turned off of 837 onto the Birmingham Bridge. This bridge was quite large compared to the other ones with six lanes and a cement barrier running down the middle dividing the traffic flow.

Once across the bridge they took an off ramp to the right, a nice downhill down slope. The old man allowed the force of gravity to create a fast and loose leg turnover, dropping his arms and allowing them to swing in counter rhythm to his legs. He had learned long ago how to run downhills fast without expending much energy—just open his stride and let the natural laws of physics take over. He noticed Jan slipping behind but figured he'd catch up on the flat. At the end of the ramp, signs directed the half marathoners to turn left onto Forbes Avenue for their final two miles back to downtown Pittsburgh and the finish line. The marathoners made a right up Forbes Avenue where they would greet the most challenging hill on the course.

The hill started at about mile twelve. The old man checked his watch: 1:34:51. They were ten seconds ahead of pace. The incline started gradually but then increased to a moderate grade.

"How are you doing?" the old man asked.

"I can definitely feel this hill."

The old man could tell Jan's breathing had become more labored. "Once we get to the top we're halfway home."

"Yeah. I'll be glad when we get up there. It's starting to heat up. I'm sweating like a fat guy at a disco."

They had been running for more than an hour and a half. The temperature had risen four or five degrees since the start. "Must be in the low sixties."

"And there's no clouds to give us a break from the sun."

As they ran under an overpass, the old man definitely felt the difference the shade made. A few seconds later they broke into the sunshine again. He noticed Jan slipping back. He slowed his pace slightly.

"Don't slow down for me," Jan said. "You're having a helluva race. I'll try to catch you on the downhill side."

"Okay. Hang in there, buddy."

"I will."

Jan is in trouble, the old man thought. He's falling off pace and we're not halfway yet. He wanted to run negative splits. If he's feeling bad already, that will be difficult to do. I still feel good, though. Am I dreaming or is this truly happening? He listened to himself breathe and felt each foot as it struck the ground and pushed off. No, I am not dreaming. I am almost halfway through my first marathon and feeling great. All of those long Sunday runs must be paying off. There is a boy and a beautiful woman waiting for me at the finish line to cheer me on. I am not dreaming, but now I am on my own.

At the top of the hill the old man gazed down Forbes Avenue and noticed a tall building rising up where the road receded to its vanishing point. He figured it had to be one of Pitt University's buildings. Now he was passing through Pitt Panther country. The street was lined with stores, fast food restaurants, parking garages, and apartment buildings. To his left he saw three tall circular towers with windows creating vertical stripes down their sides. Probably dorms for the college kids, he reasoned. Then he ran under an enclosed skywalk with the words "University of Pittsburgh – founded 1787" in golden letters on the side. The skywalk provided a safe way to get across the busy three-lane street. The old man never went to college, not because he lacked intelligence, but because no one ever planted the expectation of higher education within him. Like most of his classmates in the Ohio Valley, he entered the blue-collar workforce without questioning the drudgery of the next thirty-five years.

He neared the tall building he had noticed a half mile back. The bottom of it resembled an elaborately designed church with two red double doors. The sign on the building identified it as the Stephen Foster Memorial. He had never heard of Stephen Foster but figured he was an important fellow. Behind the church-like structure the building rose up thirty or more stories. The old man got dizzy looking up at it so he refocused on the road ahead of him.

He didn't keep focused on the street for very long because a dinosaur caught his eye to his right—a life-size brontosaurus. He

93

immediately recognized the building in front of which the brontosaurus stood—the Carnegie Museum of Natural History. He had visited the museum several times throughout his life. It was a place he could spend hours exploring, filled with displays, artifacts, taxidermied animals, dinosaur bones, and relics from the great past civilizations of the world. The architecture resembled an immense Greek temple with statues of scholars and philosophers stationed at the doors and gods and goddesses peering over the high balconies. He felt as though he had ascended Mount Olympus. Immediately after passing the museum he spotted the thirteen-mile marker. He made a quick left, ran a few blocks and turned right on Fifth Avenue. It was downhill from here.

Why did the number 13 stick in his head? He tried not to be superstitious but it bothered him whenever he saw it. He glanced at his bib number—1371. Was it an omen? So far his luck had been very good. He had run a great pace for thirteen miles. He checked his watch: 1:45:15. Better than he expected. The last thirteen miles was mostly downhill and flat. The way he felt at this juncture in the race, he may even run negative splits. Forget unlucky thirteen he told himself. He would make his own luck. Focus on the task ahead.

The road gradually slanted downward. On the sidewalk to the right he noticed a man standing alone in front of a large redbrick church and playing an acoustic guitar. With a bluesy voice he sang a song about running on empty and running behind. The old man picked up his pace, telling himself to take advantage of the downhill, but more than that he wanted to get out of earshot of the singer's words.

For several miles he trotted along through the neighborhoods on the southeast side of Pittsburgh. He welcomed the shade from the many oak and maple trees that lined the streets. These boroughs had names like Oakland, Shadyside, Latimer, and Homewood with well-kept, moderate-sized houses. The stress on his body increased with the heat, making it challenging to keep a 7:55 mile pace going, but there were very few hills to break his rhythm, and if he edged up

94

over eight minutes a mile, so what. He was still on track to obliterate the Boston qualifying time.

Without Jan beside him, his mind drifted in and out of random thoughts. Certain objects or sights would trigger a memory or an idea. He spotted a sign in front of a three-story, brick building that identified the place as THE ELLIS SCHOOL. This reminded him of an old training partner whose last name was Ellis. They had run interval workouts together on a regular basis before his severe sciatica problem started. He hadn't talked to the friend in a long time, but the memories of running hard mile intervals on First Street were fresh in his mind as if they had run yesterday. Then, knowing the building was a school, he brooded over his own lack of education. If he had it all to do over again, he would have gone to college to become a teacher and a coach. Helping Manny develop into a good distance runner was one of the joys of his life. Certainly, he would have been good at working with kids. He wondered what kind of talents remained dormant within him because he never pursued higher learning or developed his mental abilities. Music? Art? Writing? He would never know. You can't change who you are, he told himself. You can't go back in time and redo those years. All you have is today. Now he understood that he was the determiner of his fate. Was it too late? No! Today he would prove that. I may not have a lot of years left, he told himself, but I'm going to make them count.

When he saw the sixteen mile marker, he realized he needed to down the last gel pack. Several blocks ahead he spied the next water station. His throat was definitely much drier now than eight miles back. He ripped the pack from the pin and tore off the top. The ranks of runners had been weeded out by the half marathon making it easier to drift over to the tables and snatch a cup from one of the volunteers. He slowed down this time to make sure the water didn't slosh out and miss his mouth. He managed to swallow most of the liquid this time. Now the gel pack. He squeezed the bottom, and a huge glob spewed into his mouth. He tried to gulp it down but the slimy stuff got stuck at the back of his throat. He gagged, shortening his stride. Someone called out, "Are you okay?" He stopped and coughed. A heavy-set man handed him a cup of water. He choked, cleared his throat, spit, and then downed the water like a sailor finishing off a glass of beer.

"Thanks!" he called back to the man as he took off again.

"Are you sure you're alright?"

He raised his hand and gave the okay sign by using his thumb and index finger to form an "O." *That one about killed me*, he thought, *but I'm still alive and kicking.* He checked his watch: 2:07:15. *Still under pace and not feeling bad.* His legs had no zing in them, but they weren't heavy. His breathing was more noticeable but not labored. *I'm doing fine. Everything is normal. This is how I'm supposed to feel at sixteen miles. Bring on the last ten miles. I'm heading down the home stretch!*

The sun, now higher in the sky, lit the road and neighborhood with bright intensity. There were brick houses with ample lawns on both sides of the road interspersed with smaller homes, an occasional gas station. or business. To his left he noticed a reformed Presbyterian theological center, which reminded him to say a prayer: *Get me through these last ten miles, O God, and I'll read a chapter of the Bible a day. I'll even try to get to church once a month.* He wondered if God was pleased with that prayer. *Why not? It was heartfelt. He would keep his end of the bargain.* The sun beamed down upon him, but he didn't feel hot. Just warm. *Maybe that was God's sign of approval.*

The few runners he saw ahead of him made a left at the next corner onto North Braddock Avenue. Wispy cirrus clouds now appeared just above the Allegheny foothills as if God had recently brushed them onto the blue canvas. A nice breeze picked up and cooled his body. He took a deep breath of fresh air, feeling fully alive, knowing this was not a dream. A little over a mile later, right after passing the eighteen mile marker, the first sciatica pain hit him.

𝓏𝓏𝓏𝓏𝓏

At first he ignored it. He kept telling himself it was normal to have some pain in the lower right leg after running eighteen miles at a good pace. To distract himself he focused on the runners around him. Not far ahead he spotted a shirtless, light-skinned man with muscular arms and legs and a shaved head. He wasn't bulky, but his pale complexion seemed to exaggerate his well-defined physique. Usually, men who pumped iron to look good also wanted bronzed skin. A lot of them spent time in tanning salons like women. In the bright sunshine this guy looked like a ghost with muscles. Then it occurred to him that the man might be an albino. He had seen very few albinos in his life. Didn't they have pink eyes? He wanted to catch up and look, but the man was slowly pulling away.

A female runner pulled up beside him. She had dark brown hair gathered up by a purple band into a long ponytail that bounced with every stride. The old man guessed she was in her mid-thirties and quite fit.

"How far to the finish?" She asked.

"We are almost at the nineteen mile mark. About seven miles to go."

"I saw you are limping slightly. Are you okay?"

"A little pain in my lower right leg. Hopefully, it's nothing. How do you feel?"

"Tired. My training partner took off on me a few miles back. Said he felt good, so he left me. Do you mind if I run with you?"

"Not at all. I don't want to slow you down, though."

"I'm just trying to finish."

"Me too."

To their left a man dressed in a blue racing outfit shrieked and grabbed his hamstring. He limped to a stop and plopped down on the curb, audibly crying.

The girl gasped. "Can you believe that? Seven miles to go and he ripped a hammy."

"That has to be heartbreaking."

The poor man's visible agony reconnected the old man with his pain. It felt exactly like the pain he had experienced twenty years ago when pressure on his sciatic nerve referred the dull aching to the outside of his lower right leg. He feared what would come next. It was inevitable.

For a mile and a half he and the girl ran together around the northeast side of the city, passing by Highland Park and the city zoo. When they turned left on Negley Avenue, he knew they were heading southeast again in the direction of the Golden Triangle. Could he hold on for six more miles? The pain on the side of his leg had increased and crept up into his calf. Twenty years ago he had ignored it and kept running. That was a major mistake. Eventually it climbed into his hamstring and buttock. Then came the loss of feeling and the incredible amount of damage to the muscles and tendons. Without proper nerve conduction, everything pulled and tore apart.

Suddenly he felt a jolt into his hamstring as if a shark had taken a chunk out of his leg. "I've got to stop!" he yelped.

The girl glanced back, her blue eyes saddened. "Maybe I'll see you at the finish."

"I hope so."

The old man leaned over and massaged his hamstring. Then he knelt down and rubbed his calf. Runners passed him on both sides. The pain eased. More importantly, there was no numbness. Maybe there was still hope. He knew he wouldn't be able to break 3:30, but perhaps he could still complete the course in a decent time. He decided to try walking at a fast pace. The pain still needled the side of his lower leg, but it didn't hurt nearly as much as it did just a few minutes before. He limped considerably as he walked, favoring the leg as much as possible. When he got to the twenty-one mile mark he checked his watch: 2:53:31. Even with the delay for stopping and walking, he was only about three and a half minutes behind his goal pace. The pain continued to ease. Could he start running again?

"Angelo!" cried someone from behind him.

He turned to see Jan coming his way. He decided to try running with him.

"What's the matter? Did you hit the wall?"

"No. Sciatica. I'll try to hang with you as long as I can. When the pain shoots up my leg into my hamstring, I will have to stop."

"What a bad break. You were having such a great race. You were on pace to break 3:30."

"I know. And I feel good other than the leg pain. But I haven't given up hope. I'll keep pushing myself to the finish."

"The heat got to me. I'm behind Boston qualifying pace for my age. There's no way I can make up the difference in these last few miles. I'm feeling zapped."

"I'm sorry. I know you had your heart set on Boston."

"It's almost seventy degrees out here. I think I could have qualified on a cooler day."

"There will be more marathons to run."

They turned right on Liberty Avenue, and the old man spotted the twenty-two mile sign about fifty yards ahead. This was the same street the race started on. The pain bolted up through his calf and hamstring again. This time numbness tingled his leg. He stumbled to a stop.

Jan slowed and turned around. "Do you need help?"

"No. Keep going. There's nothing you can do."

"I'll see you at the finish." Jan turned and ran on.

About half his leg was numb as if he had slept on it wrong. Pain jolted into his calf, hamstring, and lower back. He leaned on his knees. "Ay!" he said aloud. It felt like someone had driven spikes through him in those three spots. A shadow crossed him, and he peered up.

"Are you hurt?" asked a stocky man dressed in white scrubs. He had short black hair shaved on the sides and a goatee.

"I've lost feeling in my leg," the old man groaned.

"We can help you." The man in white pointed to the building on the right side of the street. White letters on a green awning identified the place as the Western Pennsylvania Hospital. "John! Get that wheelchair just inside the door!"

A red haired man, also clad in white scrubs, nodded and stepped under the awning, triggering the automatic doors.

"We're a couple of nurses on break. Decided to step out and watch the race for a few minutes."

Now the old man's leg and crotch area had gone completely numb.

"Where's the pain?" asked the stocky man in white.

"I've lost feeling in my right leg. The pain started in my right calf and shot up into my lower back."

"That's not good. Sounds like you severely pinched the sciatic nerve"

The front doors of the hospital separated again and the red-haired man appeared pushing a wheelchair. He rolled it to middle of the street.

"Sit down," the stocky man said. "Let's see if we can take some pressure off that sciatic nerve."

The old man sat in the chair and the red-haired man wheeled him to the sidewalk. Feeling slowly trickled back into his leg.

"What's the problem?" the red-haired man asked.

"Pretty serious," the stocky man said. "He's lost feeling in his leg. If that sciatic nerve gets damaged or severed, he's in big trouble."

The redhead nodded and knelt in front of the old man. He pinched his right big toe. "Can you feel that?"

The old man nodded. "I'm starting to get feeling back."

"Look up at the sky," the redhead said. "I'm going to touch your leg several times in different places. You tell me when I touch you."

The old man peered into the sky. Cirrus clouds drifted high across the blue expanse. He wondered if the man was touching him. He didn't feel anything. Then he barely felt his light touch on the inside of his calf. "There. I felt it." Then he sensed the brush of the man's fingers on the inside of his thigh. "Yes. I can feel it."

The redhead stood and shook his head. "The inside's okay but the outside of your leg is still numb."

"Angelo!" someone yelled.

The old man shifted his focus to the street.

Jack Silvers ran past pointing his finger at him. "I told you so!"

The old man instinctively tried to rise to his feet, but the redhead pushed him back down.

"Stay where you are. Your condition is very serious."

"But the feeling is coming back," the old man pleaded. "The pain is almost gone."

The stocky man put his hand on the old man's shoulder. "Listen. If you try to finish the race, you could permanently damage that sciatic nerve. Do you want to be crippled for life?"

The old man shook his head.

"We're going to take you to the ER and have you checked out. You need to get your lower spine X-rayed."

The old man felt like crying. What bad luck. He realized he had violated his luck by choosing to race too far. He slumped in the chair, and the stocky man wheeled him through the front door of the hospital. Running kills me, he thought, exactly as it keeps me alive. And the boy keeps me alive. He peered down the hallway and spied the Emergency Room sign. He would probably be kept there for hours as they X-rayed, prodded, and tested him. What about Manny and Rita? How will they know what happened? Jack Silvers' voice echoed in the back of his mind: I told you so! No, the old man thought. I can't let this happen.

The old man bolted out of the wheelchair and spun around.

"What are you doing?" the stocky man demanded.

"I'm going to finish the race."

"Please, sit down," the redhead said, reaching out and clasping his arm.

The old man tried to pull away, but the nurse had a strong grip. He reached down, made a fist, and threw a roundhouse right. The punch caught the redhead squarely in the nose. He released the old man's arm and clasped his face, blood spurting between his fingers. The old man shot down the hallway toward the entrance.

"You bastard!" the redhead yelled.

The automatic doors separated, and the old man flew onto the street and into the flow of runners. The numbness had faded, but the pain on the lower outside of his leg was still noticeable. A surge of adrenaline had supercharged his body, and he ran down Liberty Avenue at a good pace, barely limping. Perhaps the five minute rest was enough to relieve the pressure on the sciatic nerve. Could he make it through four more miles? Think about something cheerful, he said to himself. Every minute that passes you are closer to the finish line. At the hospital he had almost given up hope. It's silly not to hope. Was it a sin not to hope? He wasn't sure.

Perhaps it was a sin to run the marathon knowing his history of sciatica problems. God had given him many good years of racing the shorter distances. Choosing to run the marathon was putting God to the test. His pride had made him do it. He wanted to prove to the boy and to himself he could run the distance and qualify for Boston. He wanted to show everyone that he was a true distance runner. But then again, it seemed that almost everything was a sin. How would he know what is a sin and what is not a sin? There are people with seminary degrees who could answer those questions much better than he. Quit thinking about sin, he told himself.

He wished he wouldn't have hit the male nurse in the nose. That probably was a sin. But what choice did he have? The jackass wouldn't let him go. He had no right to prevent him from returning to the race. That's my decision, the old man told himself. No one decides that for me.

He glanced up to see the twenty-three mile marker. He couldn't believe it: only three miles to go. He had been running at a good pace for about a mile, and the pain had slowly been increasing, but it was still not unbearable. Until it became unbearable, he would keep that pace. Not too far ahead he spied a runner wearing a black racing top and ball cap—Jack Silvers. He was catching the coach. The old man figured he ran the last mile at a seven minute pace, and Silvers ran about an eight minute pace. He pulled alongside his rival.

"I've returned from the dead," the old man said.

Silvers appeared startled, as if he'd seen a ghost. He picked up his pace, but the old man kept stride.

"Angelo, I see you are limping. Is it your sciatica?"

"Yes. Back at the hospital I almost gave up hope, but then the pain subsided. I decided to try and finish."

"I think you're making . . . a mistake."

"You are not me."

"Listen, . . . a permanent injury . . . isn't worth finishing one marathon."

The old man could hear Silvers struggling for each breath between his words. "You may be right. But I'm gaining confidence."

"Don't risk it."

"Sorry, Coach, but this pace is a little slow for me." The old man quickened his stride, and Silvers fell behind.

🏃🏃🏃🏃🏃

The pain did not become unbearable until mile twenty-four. But the old man did not stop this time. The sharp teeth of torment sunk deeply into his calf and then his hamstring. Another bit into his buttock and a fourth into his lower back. His running form broke apart, but he staggered on like a soldier riddled with bullets trying to make a final charge. *What can I do? I won't give up. I will run until I die.* Every step sent agony through his body. His pace dropped down to a slow jog. When his right leg and crotch went completely numb, He could not feel his foot contact the ground. This made it very difficult to keep his balance. With horrified expressions, the spectators watched him reel and teeter and totter. He assumed he looked like one of the marauding dead from the many zombie movies filmed on location in Pittsburgh.

Not only did everything hurt with excruciating intensity, but the exhaustion of the miles finally weighed upon him. He wanted to stop, crumple to the ground, and expire, but he kept putting one foot in front of the other.

"Angelo!" a familiar voice called. It was Silvers. "It looks like you are running on empty!" The coach passed him, glanced back over his shoulder, and shook head. "I told you so!"

103

Now the old man knew the fight was useless. He wondered how much damage he had already done to his body. He made a few more steps before his lack of feeling and balance caused him to stumble to the ground. Two men in the crowd stepped forward to help him, but he waved them off.

"No! Don't touch me."

They backed away.

The old man began to crawl, dragging his right leg. He could not feel it scuffing against the asphalt. After several minutes he glanced down and noticed the skin had worn off his knee and shin. The blood seeped out leaving a crimson trail, but he kept crawling. He felt like a cockroach that had been stepped on but still alive, inching its way back to some dark corner to die. Sweat burned his eyes, the asphalt grated his palms, but he kept moving forward. As the minutes passed, he noticed a tingling up and down the lame leg. Was he regaining feeling? He peered up to see the twenty-five mile marker. He stopped crawling, leaned back on his haunches, shifted all his weight to his good leg, and struggled to rise his feet.

He bent over and massaged his hamstring. Reaching behind, he rubbed his buttock and lower back. Slowly the numbness went away, and he felt the searing rawness of his knee and shin. He tried taking a step, and realized he had some control over his right leg. He walked with a limp. He feared trying to run again. His mind went blank for a while—no thoughts or feelings of any kind. Then he longed for his bed. Lying down would be a great thing. He knew he was beaten. But I will not be defeated, he told himself. The bed can wait. I will finish. I may be destroyed, but I will not be defeated.

"Angelo!" a familiar voice called.

He squinted into the crowd lined along the orange snow fence and spotted the boy.

"You have a half mile to go!" The boy tapped his wristwatch. "You can still qualify for Boston!"

The old man checked his watch: 3:49:45. The boy was right. If he made it to the finish line in five minutes he would qualify. The old man tried jogging. It felt like he had strained every muscle in his right leg, but he gritted his teeth and hobbled as fast as he could. How could qualifying still be possible? Then he realized what had happened. For the first eighteen miles he had run under eight minutes a mile. That gave him a huge cushion. In suffering the hell of the last eight miles, he had forgotten about the surplus of time he had built up.

After a couple hundred yards the numbness threatened again. He knew if he had to crawl, he would not make it in time. He stopped, shook out his leg, and rubbed the areas that had no feeling.

"Come on, Angelo! You've got to keep going!" Manny shouted. The boy was running too, making his way through the crowd.

The old man started again, pushing himself as fast as he could go through the pain. Every time he stopped to shake out the numbness, the boy would catch up and cheer him on. He stopped three more times. His vision blurred, but he knew the finish line was less than a hundred yards away. The leg went completely numb again, but he kept flailing his arms and swinging the leg, lunging haltingly forward. As soon as he crossed the orange finish stripe he crumpled to his knees. Two aids rushed to him, each grabbing an arm. They bore most of his weight as they lifted him onto his feet and led him off to the side, out of the way of the other finishers.

"I'll be fine," he said. "Let me rest here a minute." He rubbed his eyes, trying to focus on their faces. As his vision cleared, Manny's face appeared between the two aids.

"I'll help him. I'm his best friend," Manny said.

A security officer rushed over to them. "Young man, I saw you jump over that fence. You are not allowed in this restricted area. Runners and officials only!"

But Manny had already ducked under the old man's arm, helping him to stand.

"Yes sir," the boy said. "I'm leaving now. But Angelo's coming with me."

The old man, even in his tremendous pain, could not help smiling. With the boy's assistance, he hobbled through the finish line area. A young blonde girl wearing a red t-shirt with the marathon logo on the front stepped up to them and slipped a yellow and black ribbon around the old man's neck. The old man held up the heavy triangular medal attached to the ribbon and inspected it. The silhouette of three runners appeared in relief at the bottom and a yellow bridge crossed the top with the words "Pittsburgh Marathon" in between the images. He kept eyeing the yellow bridge.

"Do you want to go to the medical tent?" Manny asked.

"No. I just want to go home."

Manny pointed to a bench along the sidewalk. "Sit here and I will get you a bottle of water."

"Make it two bottles," the old man said.

Manny helped lower him to the bench and then jogged back toward the people handing out bottles of water. The old man felt tingling in the bad leg. Was the feeling returning? I may have to drive home using my left foot, he thought. Or perhaps Rita will volunteer to drive. But where was Rita? He panned the area. Then he heard her voice.

"Manny! Manny, come here!" She stood on the other side of the orange snow fence about forty yards away.

Manny approached her carrying two bottles of water. He stopped in front of her, and they talked for about a minute. The old man could not hear their conversation. Then the boy turned and walked toward him. Rita disappeared into the crowd.

Manny handed him a bottle of water.

"Where's Rita going?" The old man twisted off the cap and took a swig.

"She's taking care of Coach Silvers."

"What?"

"She said that Coach Silvers is feeling sick and dizzy. She's worried he will not be able to drive himself home."

The old man took a few seconds to process the boy's words. "Hmmmph. She's not riding back with us, is she?"

The boy shook his head.

The old man bent over, leaned his elbows on his knees, and stared at the ground.

"Can I get you anything else?" Manny said.

The old man shook his head.

"I'll be back in a minute. Stay here."

"I'm not moving," the old man groaned.

As Manny turned and headed toward a coffee shop a few paces down the street, a thin man with long brown hair and a big nose stopped him. Because the man was wearing a racing number, Manny figured he had also run the marathon.

The long haired guy pointed to the old man. "Is Angelo all right?"

"He's in a lot of pain, but he'll be okay. He's a tough old man."

"He ran with me through thirteen miles and then he pulled away. We were averaging under 7:55 per mile. Too bad the sciatica hit him. He probably would have placed in his age group."

"I believe it," the boy said. He turned to go, but a woman stepped in front of him. She had long brown hair clasped into a ponytail and bright blue eyes.

"Do you know that man on the bench?"

"Yes. He's my best friend."

"We ran together for a couple miles. Tell him how sorry I am."

"I will."

The woman smiled and walked away.

Manny headed down the street and into the coffee shop. He ordered a large cup of the bold morning brew, paid for it with his own money, and walked back to the old man.

"Here." He handed the old man the coffee. "I know you like your coffee more than water."

"Thanks." The old man put down the bottle of water and took the cup, opened the flip-top, and sipped. "They beat me, Manny. They truly did."

"The marathon did not beat you."

"No. Other things took away my leg and my woman." The old man unpinned his number from his racing top. "Here. Throw this away for me."

"Don't you want it?"

"No. It brought me bad luck."

"To hell with luck," the boy said. "You don't need luck to be a good runner."

"My running days are over."

"What are you talking about? You have a lot yet to teach me."

"Coach Silvers will teach you. He had no problem beating me today."

"But Coach Silvers did not qualify for the Boston Marathon today."

"He didn't?"

"No. Rita told me he missed it by a minute. But you did."

"What?"

"Yes. You ran 3:54:55. You made it by five seconds. I thought you knew."

"No. My vision became blurry at the end. I couldn't see the finish clock or my watch."

"You have eleven months to prepare. I will train with you."

"But what will your father say?"

"What can he say? You qualified for the Boston Marathon and Coach Silvers didn't. You must heal up quickly. There is much for you to teach me and a lot of miles to run."

"But my leg is severely injured."

"The Witch Doctor will help you. Did you suffer much during the race?"

"Plenty."

"But you didn't quit."

"Of course not."

"And I will not let you quit now that you qualified for Boston."

𝗑𝗑𝗑𝗑𝗑

Later that afternoon shortly after they had arrived home, the boy took thumbtacks and pinned the old man's race number to the bulletin board that hung on his bedroom wall. Above the number months ago he had pinned a sheet of notebook paper with his track goal written on it: *Break the school record for the 3200 meter run—under 9:11.* He went into the bathroom and opened the medicine cabinet. He found a bottle of aspirin, some rubbing alcohol, and a tube of pain relief cream. He carried the items down to the kitchen and stuffed them into a paper lunch bag.

Then he walked the few blocks to the old man's house, climbed the steep front steps, and turned the knob on the door. It was unlocked as usual. The house was silent, except for the subtle sound of the old man's rhythmic breathing. He entered the living room and saw that the old man had fallen asleep on his recliner. A running magazine lay open across his bare chest. The boy sat on the couch next to the recliner and watched his best friend sleep. His calf muscles twitched and the blood on his knee and shin had dried to a dark red. The boy noticed how thin his eyelids were and how his eyes moved rapidly under them.

𝄖𝄖𝄖𝄖𝄖

The old man was dreaming about running along the beach with the wild horses.

About the Author

Joe C. Ellis grew up in the Ohio Valley. A native of Martins Ferry, Ohio, he attended West Liberty State College in West Virginia and went on to earn his Master's Degree in education from Muskingum College in New Concord, Ohio. He has been employed by Martins Ferry City Schools for the last thirty-four years where he currently teaches art and computer graphics at Martins Ferry High School. He also has been lay preaching for the Presbyterian Church U.S.A. for the last twenty-two years. He pastors two churches in the Martins Ferry area, the Scotch Ridge Presbyterian Church and the Colerain Presbyterian Church.

His writing career began in 2001 with the publication of his first novel, *The Healing Place*. In 2007 he began the Outer Banks Murder Series with the publication of *Murder at Whalehead* and in 2010 *Murder at Hatteras*. The popularity of this series continues to grow with his 2012 installment, *Murder on the Outer Banks*. The next novel in this series, *Murder at Ocracoke*, is scheduled for August of 2014

Joe credits family vacations on the Outer Banks with the inspiration for these stories. Joe and his wife, Judy, have three children and three grandsons. Although the kids have flown the nest, they get together often and always make it a priority to vacation on the Outer Banks whenever possible. He comments, "It's a place on the edge of the world, a place of great beauty and sometimes danger—the ideal setting for murder mysteries."

One of Joe's passions is distance running. *Murder on the Outer Banks* opens with a 5K footrace in which an older man runs to victory against much younger competition. In the last several years Joe has posted 5k times and half marathon times at the national class level for his age group. Because running definitely keeps him younger physically and mentally, he enjoyed writing a novel with these themes as important threads in the plot. Joe hopes to continue to write stories set on the Outer Banks and run along its beaches for many years to come.

His latest novel, *The Old Man and the Marathon*, was inspired and modeled after Ernest Hemingway's *The Old Man and the Sea*. Joe would like to write a sequel to this novel called *The Old Man and the Boston Marathon*. Before he writes the book, though, he wants to qualify for the Boston Marathon and actually run it. In 2009 he ran the Pittsburgh Marathon and qualified for the Boston. However, time slipped by on him and he missed the cut off date to secure a spot in the race. If you enjoyed this novel and would like to read the sequel, please let Joe know by emailing him at joecellis@comcast.net.

Joe C. Ellis finishing the Pittsburgh Marathon – May 3, 2009

Novels by Joe C. Ellis

Ohio Valley Mystery Series:

The Healing Place ISBN=978-0-9796655-1-6
The First Shall Be Last ISBN=978-0-9796655-2-3
One Season of Our Lives ISBN=978-0-9796655-5-4

The Outer Banks Murder Series:

Murder at Whalehead ISBN=978-0-9796655-0-9
Murder at Hatteras ISBN=978-0-9796655-3-0
Murder on the Outer Banks ISBN=978-0-9796655-4-7
Murder at Ocracoke (to be published in August of 2014)

All of the books are available in hardcopy or ebook versions for the Kindle or Nook. Murder on the Outer Banks is also available as an audiobook at Amazon.com and Audible.com

ISBN 978-0-9796655-6-1

51299

Printed in the United States of America

9 780979 665561

www.ingramcontent.com/pod-product-compliance
Lightning Source LLC
Chambersburg PA
CBHW020147180626
46810CB00004B/1775